DALLIANCES

SPRING 2025

FOREWORD

W E ARE EXCITED TO SHARE our first *Dalliances* romance anthology. The anthology features a wide variety of stories, including some that involve selkies, same sex couples, and even a throuple.

Our authors come from all walks of life and we are thrilled to have them with us. We hope that you will thoroughly enjoy all of the short stories we've included as much as we enjoyed reading, selecting, and editing them.

Sitting down to write a romance is a very special process. Usually the author has a "story seed"—an idea of what they want to write about. Sometimes, when the story is finished, it's gone in the intended direction but in other cases, the story has taken on a life of its own.

Sitting down to read a romance story is special too, as we escape into a story that whisks us away. We hope that these stories will capture your attention and interest. The authors we have included have fresh and fabulous stories to share with you, including some that are fun and quirky. As you read, we hope that you will enjoy the diversity of the stories as much as we did.

Cupid's Arrow Publishing Editorial Team

HEAT LEVEL INDEX

LOW

Light
Romance

MEDIUM

Some
Passionate
Action

HOT

Some
Hot and Heavy
Action

CONTENTS

Unexpected Reunion 1

Far, Far Away...19

Two Dolls and a Vinyoc 33

A Pigeon in Winterset 51

Iris Immortal...63

The Date..79

Of Leather and Wool......................................89

Fixer Upper...103

Where I Belong 119

When We Say Nothing At All.....................127

Firebugs 143

My Way Back to You 163

UNEXPECTED REUNION

J. M. de la Torre

DESPITE THE FORECAST'S "low chance of precipitation," dense gray clouds cracked open and slammed Uptown with a relentless sheet of rain, sparing no one in the city streets below. Not even the pedestrians who had been clever enough to grab some protective gear before starting their day, like Estrella. She thrived on being prepared for any occasion, especially on stormy days. She hunched beneath her umbrella and nudged her blue-framed glasses back up her nose, determined to get to her destination as dry as possible.

Unfortunately for Estrella, the weather gods had chosen chaos. She rounded the corner and groaned as a gust of wind snapped one of the umbrella's metal ribs like a twig, the loose panel flapping and splashing more water in her direction. As if that wasn't enough, the weather's continued audacity forced her to tilt her broken polka-dotted shield at a near perpendicular angle to fight back against the whipping winds. *I'm really starting to regret getting up this early in the morning.*

Once she trudged past her go-to bakery, which she was already planning on visiting after her morning exercise, her sights landed on her Uncle Rodrigo's crowning jewel, La Perla. Stretching twenty stories high, his luxury hotel sat near the heart of Uptown. It came with all the amenities, including a 24/7 gym his favorite niece could use whenever she wanted.

Upon finding cover beneath the hotel's awning, she exhaled a sigh of relief and pushed through the revolving door into the double-page spread of an interior design magazine. Even though it was dressed in high-end furnishings and light fixtures that were more expensive than her college education, the lobby still had traces of its late 19th century origin, her favorite detail being the marble inlay medallion blooming across the center of the room. Most guests walked past it in favor of checking in at the front desk, but not Estrella. Regardless of how many times she had seen it and traced the lines of the starburst with the tip of her foot, she couldn't help but to stop in her tracks to admire it.

Years ago, Rodrigo encouraged her to stand in the middle of the shining star and told her to make a wish. "The universe is always listening," he said, his calm voice giving her the impression he had done it before with resounding success.

None of her wishes ever came true, but that didn't stop her from trying multiple times throughout the years. Even now, as she stood at the golden center, facing the northern cardinal point and the front desk, she closed her eyes and mentally whispered her heart's latest desire. *I hope you're listening this time, universe. I've been putting in a lot of effort at work, but no dice so far. A little assistance would be greatly appreciated.*

"You're dripping all over my lobby."

That was not the response she was seeking from the almighty universe, but she smiled all the same as she turned west toward her uncle, the soles of her bright yellow rain boots squeaking against the polished floor. "Tío."

"Sobrina," he said, his scruffy, peppered beard looking more trimmed and styled than usual. He also donned a tailored burgundy suit, a sure sign he was expecting fancy guests today. Dripping water on his floor was probably the last thing he needed, but he approached her with a genuine smile—not one of those practiced grins he summoned for customer service—and a hug.

Given their sandy complexions, tangled manes of chestnut hair, and inviting amber eyes, anyone who didn't know them would have guessed they were father and daughter. The assumption happened so often from various hotel guests, they stopped correcting people a long time ago and went along with it.

"Another early morning at the gym?"

Estrella removed her Queen City Royals FC cap—one of the many items she owned of her favorite soccer team—and ruffled her bushy ponytail to get rid of any lingering water droplets. "Yeah, I need it."

She didn't need the gym for any of the usual reasons, like keeping in shape or increasing endurance. The truth was Estrella hated exercising, but the act of running on a treadmill, lifting weights, or doing anything else that felt like muscle torture helped her focus and think.

He nodded in understanding and reached out for the mop one of his workers brought over. She loved that about her uncle. He wasn't above doing menial tasks, even while wearing a designer suit.

"While you're here, I've got good news and bad news," he said as he wiped the water trail away.

"What's the good news?" She always liked having the good news first in any situation. She equated it to eating dessert first, which she did often.

"Darlene is working again." Estrella pumped a fist through the air in victory. Rodrigo had been restoring the hotel's four elevators in phases, making sure they were operating at modern standards while also keeping some of their 1920s art deco charm. One of the elevators—the one she dubbed Darlene—refused to function and opted to break down at inconvenient times.

If he and his team managed to get the elevator back up and running again, which had been a thorn in his side for almost a year, her curiosity spiked. "What's the bad news, then?"

His mopping paused long enough to serve her a wince. "The opposing team in tonight's game against the Queen City

Royals is staying here. I didn't tell you before because I didn't want to upset you."

She had prepared herself for the chaotic thunderstorm ranging outside, but she was not at all prepared for the missile of information her uncle had just dropped, her fingers fanning out over her chest as if to keep her heart from exploding. While she was dead set against supporting other teams, this news wasn't as dreadful as her uncle led her to believe, mainly because she had been following the career of one Golden Gate United FC player for the past decade. Some would have called her obsessed, but she considered herself dedicated and loyal with a dash of occasionally unhinged.

Her head swiveled in every direction as if expecting him to round a corner and make a dramatic entrance back into her life, but apart from Pamela, the bright-eyed desk clerk who was ready to receive new guests, the lobby remained empty.

"They're having breakfast in the event space, so try not to scratch their eyes out. It's bad for business."

Located a few floors above them, the event space had some of the best views of Uptown Park and its pond. It also had its own kitchen with a separate entrance to the event space. She could pose as one of the staff members—it wouldn't be the first time—and bypass any security, but then what? She'd awkwardly reintroduce herself and ask if he'd want to keep in touch? No, this was the unhinged part of her devotion rearing its ugly head and trying to satisfy a long-time crush. He'd probably laugh in her face, something she believed he was incapable of doing, but years under the limelight tended to change people. He could also call security before she even had a chance to explain her absurd motives. She couldn't do that to herself, but she also couldn't embarrass her uncle and destroy his reputation. *So close, yet so far.* "I won't let my allegiances land us on the front paper."

Rodrigo lifted a ringed pinky finger, a hint of a smirk on his face. "Promise?"

Pinky swears were a deep-rooted practice in her family, but the roots ran deeper with her uncle. She wrapped her pinky around his and squeezed. "I promise."

Estrella stomped her wet boots on the mop before walking around the front desk to hide her umbrella and to pick up her swipe card. She waved the piece of plastic at Rodrigo as she left the lobby and entered the short hallway of elevators. Before their restoration, the elevators' interior walls were distressed, and the metallic sculptural elements embedded on the walls and around the ceiling accumulated grime over the decades. Her uncle gave them a new lease on life, but something about the way Darlene's door opened, like it was hesitant about letting anyone in, gave her pause. Estrella considered flagging down her uncle, but one look at the time on her watch forced her to abandon that thought and enter the elevator. *Darlene's probably just getting used to this century.*

After she pressed the button for the twelfth floor, Estrella pushed aside lingering thoughts of her deranged plan and busied herself by using the elevator's mirror panels to fix her hair and reapply her lip balm. As she patted down her flyaways with little success, she shifted her focus back to work. An early morning session in the gym would help her figure out if sticking with her job for another year was worth it or if it was time to move on. She was in the middle of rubbing the balm along her bottom lip when Darlene stopped and opened her door with more confidence for the next passenger.

Estrella's stomach clenched, much like it did whenever she strapped herself into the front seat of a rollercoaster. Thrill rides brought her insurmountable levels of joy, but that didn't stop little ol' anxiety from penetrating her insides and tightening them like a fist. The guy who'd been living in her head for the past ten years, also known as her high school crush, stood in the reflection. His casual glance at the other elevators gave her the impression he was waiting for an empty ride, but she shuffled to the corner and held her breath, hoping he would reconsider.

The voices and footsteps of other soccer players grew louder by the second. When it became clear the other elevators weren't going to appear for him, he stepped inside, pressed the button for his floor, and repeatedly smashed the close button until Darlene responded. It wasn't lost on Estrella that his body language expressed an urgent need to be alone, but that didn't stop her inner giddy 14-year-old from opening her mouth.

"You're Lorenzo Denova," she said and winced at the obvious fact.

He kept his head forward, facing the rays of an etched sun on the door's mirror, while his brown eyes landed on hers through the reflection. Like the real sun, staring back was almost too much for her to bear, so she shifted her gaze to the number panel instead. "Yeah. Listen, now's not a good time for an autograph or selfie."

Estrella's mouth slackened. "No, that's not—I'm not a fan."

"Ouch," he said, a tinge of genuine hurt in his voice as he turned his head in her direction. "Thanks for your honesty?"

Her inner teen withered. "That's not what I meant."

The rest of Lorenzo's body, which was covered in a crimson tracksuit that complemented his warm beige skin and fuzzy black hair, turned to fully face her. "What did you mean, then?"

She couldn't believe she had his undivided attention after all this time. The usual sea of security guards, paparazzi, and diehard soccer enthusiasts weren't standing between them, and neither were the throngs of students from their high school days. "I mean I'm a fan with boundaries. I'm not one of those people who worships you as a god and digs around your trash to add your tooth floss to my altar."

Lorenzo cocked his head and wrinkled his nose. "That's *very* specific."

"Yeah, well, my family of crazed soccer fans has a dark and scandalous past."

The soft chuckle that followed took her by surprise. She wasn't particularly good at making others laugh. In fact, her family always grumbled whenever she graced them with one of her dad jokes. She wanted to savor his response, but Darlene interrupted.

Metal grated against metal. The frictional screech assaulted her ears and caused her teeth to ache. The elevator walls shook as the cabin halted abruptly, and the lights flickered, threatening to envelope them in darkness.

Estrella breathed easy when the power didn't give out. *This is definitely not how I wanted this reunion to happen.* She shot Lorenzo a glance and recognized his tense expression. He usually wore it whenever a referee made a bad call or when an opposing team scored a goal. She didn't have time to figure out whether that was better than looking terrified.

Instead, she inched closer to the panel, thumbed the emergency button, and waited for the green light to flash, an indication that her call was being received. "Tío Rodrigo, Pamela, anyone? The elevator broke down!"

After a few moments, the intercom crackled and popped like a vintage vinyl record spinning on a turntable. Her uncle's voice boomed. "Which one? Darlene?"

"Yeah. I'm also not alone here," she responded as she flashed a look in Lorenzo's direction. His eyes were closed, and he was using his knuckles to massage his temples. It didn't require any special skills to know his day wasn't off to a great start, either. "I have a Golden Gate United player, so the faster you can get it fixed, the better."

"My sincerest apologies. I'll get a maintenance team on it. We'll get you both out of there as soon as possible." The sizzling line went dead after that, leaving behind a hushed atmosphere of uncomfortable energy.

"This is just *fantastic*," Lorenzo said as he pocketed his hands in his jacket and lifted his gaze to the ceiling.

His annoyance stabbed her in the gut. "Please don't hold this against him. La Perla really is an outstanding hotel." The lack of response worried her, so she switched gears. "Here's a fun fact ... we went to high school together."

She almost broke into a small victory dance when his attention fell back on her. "You went to Farbrook High?" His eyes narrowed in disbelief. "Prove it."

Estrella took no offense at his implication of her being a liar. She suspected Lorenzo had constructed thick walls to protect himself from the public. He was a celebrity, after all. Luckily for her, she had proof dangling from her necklace. Unlike most of her friends, she loved high school. She got along with everyone, her teachers became part of her support system, and the overall experience helped her define what she wanted to do in life. And unlike most of her friends, she memorialized her school years with a piece of jewelry. Estrella pulled the silver chain from behind her shirt and presented her class ring. The ruby red stone didn't sparkle as much as it did a decade ago and the silver band showed considerable wear, but the letters surrounding the stone clearly spelled out "Farbrook High School."

He angled his body closer to inspect, giving her the opportunity to do the same. The scar on the tail-end of his left eyebrow—the result of a player's elbow jabbing his head in mid jump—was still there. His standard buzz cut hadn't changed much, either. The tattoo peeking out from underneath his neckline, however, was new. People speculated and imagined, but he kept the design and its meaning to himself, which wasn't unusual for his discreet and reserved personality. Her hand itched to uncover the mystery, but she snuffed her curiosity and snapped her attention back to the main topic. "It's okay you don't remember me. We didn't run in the same circles. You were also a year ahead of me."

"Still, pretty small world," he said as he leaned back against his side of the elevator. "What's your name?"

The simple question nearly floored her, but her neural activity recovered enough to give him an intelligible answer. "Estrella, but I go by Rella. It sounds like 'heya'." She accompanied her introduction with finger guns, a gesture embedded deep in her wonky programming.

A smile tugged at the corner of his lips. "I go by Renzo."

"Yeah, I know. You're the one who gave me the idea of going by Rella instead of Ella. It sounded cooler."

The dimple on his right cheek deepened. "Well, it's nice to meet you, *Rella*. I'm just sorry it had to happen in a broken-down elevator."

"I think it's perfect. It's a good way to get stuff off our chests before we plummet to our deaths."

"We're not going to plummet to our deaths," he said, brimming with confidence before second-guessing himself. "Right?"

Rella grimaced. "This happened about two years ago. It was all over the news. Some of the staff say they can still hear the screams."

His posture went rigid. "Are you serious?"

She wasn't a prankster by nature, so her growing grin betrayed her. "I'm kidding."

Relief washed over him, evidenced by the dissipating tension in his shoulders. She was even rewarded with one of his rare laughs. It originated somewhere in the depths of his chest and bubbled up in a pitch slightly higher than his normal deep-toned voice. Part of her wished she had recorded it.

"You got me good," he said, pressing a hand against his chest.

"Journalist, one. Pro soccer player, nil."

His lingering smile wavered. She could almost see his wall defenses reinforcing themselves. "So, you're a journalist."

"Loosely speaking. I'm a writer for a local media outlet. What I want to be is a soccer journalist, but my editors have me writing fluff pieces about the best barbecue spots in the city and the most adorable cat videos."

Renzo crossed his arms and tipped his chin up to the ceiling. "Mm, barbecue," he teased as hints of a daydream also clouded his eyes.

Rella almost snapped her fingers above his face, but her uncle's voice pierced the enclosed space and captured their attention, reeling them closer to the intercom.

"Estrella, the maintenance crew is working on it. Are you two okay?" he said, his words laced with apprehension. She knew he was worried about the potential financial consequences of trapping a Golden Gate United player in one of his elevators, but she also knew his biggest concern was their safety—and more specifically, her safety.

"Yeah, we're fine, Tío. We broke the ice and now we're getting to know each other," she replied, flashing Renzo a warm smile before averting her gaze.

"Okay. I'm going to supervise the work, so if you need anything, let Pamela know," he said, his strained tone tugging at her heart.

A brief silence drifted through the air after the call ended. She had no doubt her uncle was being hard on himself, so she pinned a note in the corner of her mind to give him extra hugs once this was all over.

"Tío means uncle, right? Are you two related?"

Rella wondered whether his basic knowledge were remnants of their high school's Spanish class with Señora Alvarez or the influence of some of his Spanish-speaking teammates. She nodded. "He's my uncle on my dad's side."

"Are you staying here?"

"No, I like to use the gym. I avoid paying a membership somewhere else and having to deal with people's judgy looks."

His dimple returned as another smile surfaced. "Judgy looks are annoying. It's nice that he lets you use it."

"Yeah, he's like a second dad to me, always being there at my side and willing to give me everything I need."

She regretted her words the instant his eyes watered over. "That's like the relationship I had with my high school coach."

The memory of a wide-shouldered man with grizzled hair and golden-brown skin took shape in her mind. "Coach Anderson?"

Jack Anderson used to treat her journalistic questions with sincerity, instead of shooing her away and recommending she find a new hobby. Her scheduled fifteen minutes with him every season always turned into a two-hour session about his "Farbrook boys." She didn't mind, since it gave her plenty of writing material. He passed away a short time ago. One month, to be exact. It didn't take a genius to connect Renzo's earlier mood with his currently bowed spine and downturned features. A month had passed by for everyone else, but she imagined it was still a fresh wound for him.

Despite Darlene's groaning, Rella switched positions and stood beside him. "I'm really sorry for your loss, Renzo. I spoke with him on occasion, even after we graduated. He had a knack for telling stories and giving life advice. He also told me he didn't like putting certain players above others, but I could tell you were one of his favorites. He was super proud of you."

Renzo's head tilted toward her, his eyes softening. "Thanks for that."

She shrugged her shoulder and dropped her gaze to the floor, too modest to receive his gratitude with direct eye contact. "You're welcome."

He knocked the side of her rain boot with his sneaker, successfully sending an electric charge up her body to power up one of her vibrant smiles. "Go back to the part about writing fluff pieces."

Her energized smile was only the tip of the iceberg. Renzo wanting to continue their previous conversation lit up her entire world like a Christmas tree. She could talk about her work for days, but instead of drowning him with her woes, she delivered the succinct version. "I hate it. I'd kill to write about soccer again, like I did in high school and college. Those were the days."

His back straightened. For a moment, she thought he was going to put space between them, but he did the opposite. He slid closer and faced her, supporting his upper arm against the wall. Rella caught a whiff of his cologne and begged her knees not to buckle. It was something from the citrus family with notes of creamy vanilla and warm sandalwood. It took all of her willpower to not lean forward and bury her nose in his jacket. "Hang on, you wrote for the school paper?"

Rella batted away the mental fog threatening to take over her senses. "I was their soccer correspondent. Why?"

Renzo's face beamed as his freckled hand reached for his wallet in his back pocket. He flipped it open, extracted a folded newspaper clipping from behind his state identification card, and offered it to her. "Did you write this?"

Her pulse quickened. *This can't be real,* she thought as her wide-eyed stare flitted between his curious face and the paper in his hand. She took it, the rosy undertones of her cheeks reddening under his watchful gaze. Her fingers unfolded the worn and torn edges of the clipping. She instantly recognized the content because she had a copy just like it in one of her scrapbooks. The top of the article featured a photograph of a younger Renzo, his leg outstretched to pass the ball to another player.

"'1-2-3 Goals! Farbrook's Pro Soccer Player in the Making Scores Incredible Victory' by E. Santiago," she read aloud before peeking back up at him. "My full name's Estrella Santiago. I wrote this in the stands after your hat-trick against Vandergreen. The security guard had to escort me out because I was the only one left, still scribbling away in my notebook. You ... you carry this in your wallet?"

"Every day since Coach Anderson showed it to me," he said, his voice cracking part of the way.

A charged silence filled the air. The reality of him holding on to something she wrote after all these years raised her internal temperature and dried her mouth out. The steady eye contact between them, leaving her breathless, also didn't help. She cleared her throat and found her voice. "I'm glad it meant something to you."

Renzo dampened his bottom lip with the tip of his tongue. "More than you know. Any chance I can get it autographed?"

Quick with the draw, Rella echoed his earlier sentiments. "Oh, I'm sorry. Now's not a good time for an autograph or selfie."

His shoulders shook with laughter. If she could add "making Renzo laugh" next to museum hopping and collecting postcards on her list of favorite hobbies, she would.

"Fair enough," he said and almost plucked the clipping out of her hands, but she dodged him, a playful smirk on her lips. Rella about-faced and positioned the article against the elevator wall, thankful she never left home without a pen in her purse. She was about to sign her name next to her byline when Renzo spoke again. "Feel free to also add your number."

A visible flush crept up her neck and ears like spilled juice across a table. "Someone's being bold."

"Hey, the universe put us in the same elevator for a reason. I'm not wasting the opportunity to get to know you after we get out of this. Alive, hopefully."

His words echoed in her head and conjured thoughts of the sunburst medallion in the lobby. Did the universe actually listen? Was this one of Rella's many wishes finally coming true? She had no evidence to support that theory, but the notion still tickled her.

She snuck an accusatory glance at him from the corner of her eye. "You wasted an opportunity before."

Renzo crossed his arms, his eyes wandering as if his brain was trying to puzzle the pieces of his past together. He came up dry. "When?"

"Your senior year, my junior year. At the annual throwback dance. You were sitting with your friends. It took me at least ten minutes to pluck up the courage to ask you for a dance. When I did, you said, 'Sorry, I don't dance. You're better off asking someone else.' You weren't rude about it or anything like that, but I walked away thinking, 'Wow, he blew his shot.'"

He chuckled and shook his head. "I guess I did."

Rella turned her attention back to the newspaper cutout. She signed her name with a sophisticated combination of squiggles she had practiced as a kid in the event she ever became famous, while Renzo checked his phone. She assumed he was getting in touch with his coaches and teammates, but a tune straight out of the 80s inundated the elevator.

She bit her lip to keep the dopey grin on her face from fully taking over. "What are you doing?"

Renzo pocketed his phone and offered his hand, his shoulders and arms appearing far more relaxed than when he first stepped into the elevator. "I owe you a dance."

"I thought you said you didn't dance," she replied, abandoning the signed clipping and her purse on the floor.

"I've learned a few things since then."

A minuscule part of her wondered if the fear of being trapped caused her to hallucinate or if Darlene's rickety stop knocked her out cold and she was unconscious on the floor. Those musings evaporated the moment she touched his hand. She never got the chance to hold it before, not even when she volunteered at his graduation ceremony and watched him spend the better part of an hour hugging friends and shaking the hands of his instructors. His palm was warm, his fingers gentle, his grip steady and reassuring. Rella ignored the pounding heartbeat growing louder in her ears as his scented clothes lured her in, his other hand snaking around her side and down to her lower back.

His voice cut through the heady fog attempting to cloud her brain again. "Was that the only time we interacted?"

Rella shook her head, her glasses easing down to the tip of her nose. "There was one other time, but it was in college."

"Don't tell me we went to the same college!"

A raspy giggle crawled out of her throat. "No, but our teams played against each other multiple times. I got permission to interview some of you before one of the games, but you took one look at me and my notebook and said—"

"I don't do interviews."

She raised her brows and studied his face for a moment. "You remember?"

"Sorry, no," he whispered, his apology accompanied by the gentle squeeze of his hand. "I just don't like interviews. I never know what to say, and I'm always afraid something will be taken out of context."

"I get it. Someone poking and prodding your brain for things you might not be prepared to answer or even want to answer? It's not easy. Depending on the person, interviews can come off as interrogations, but when I sit down with people, it's more of a conversation."

His eyes locked on hers, a mixture of curiosity and something else Rella couldn't pin down swimming around in his irises. "Do you love what you do?"

Rella inhaled a sharp breath, having asked herself that question on countless occasions, especially in the middle of sleepless nights. She brought their joined hands closer to bump her glasses back into a proper position. "Writing fluff pieces? No. Writing about the sport I love and grew up watching? Yes." She tipped her chin up and flipped the question back at him. "Do you love what you do?"

The curve of his lips turned upward. "I love it. Every inch of that field, from goal post to goal post, is where I feel most alive. I can't imagine my life without soccer."

Rella didn't know much about his childhood and what made him fall in love with the sport in the first place, but she believed him. "I pick up on that every time I watch you play. There's this I-can-do-anything aura around you. Anything within reason, of course."

Renzo's thumb drew a searing circle against her spine, rustling the butterflies in her stomach. "You still watch me play?"

A film reel of memories whirled to life in her head as her fingernails played with the short hairs at the base of his neck. One recollection featured Rella doing homework while riding an intercity bus to one of his intercollegiate matches. Those trips also included occasional plane rides when buses and trains didn't go far or fast enough. Another recollection involved her dad groaning when she stole the remote control to watch a league championship match she couldn't attend in person. The whines from her friends were even louder whenever they hung out at sports bars and restaurants with television screens. "I never miss a game."

His smile transitioned into a full-blown smirk, his dimple greeting her once more. "So, I take it you're coming to the game tonight?"

Rella sucked in her lips, unsure if he was ready for the truth, but it burrowed its way out of her mouth and into the shared space between them. "I am, but I'll be wearing a QC Royals jersey, since they're my favorite team."

His forehead wrinkled as his eyebrows shot skyward, his mouth failing to conceal his amusement. "Wow, you know how to cut deep."

She shrugged a shoulder, her glasses sliding out of place again. Regardless of the victor in the upcoming match, she was getting the best of both worlds with her favorite team and favorite player sharing the same field. "Sorry, my allegiances run pretty deep."

"I can respect that," he said, his eyes darting down to her lips. It was a fleeting moment that poured a jar of toasty tingles down the center of her back. "I have an idea for you."

Rella nipped her tongue, her equivalent of a pinch to the arm, to focus on the change in subject. "What kind of idea?"

"The making-you-a-soccer-journalist kind."

Her shoulders straightened and her hand itched to readjust her glasses, but she disregarded the impulse. "I'm listening."

"The whole me-not-liking-interviews thing, I'll make an exception. For you, and only you."

Rella blinked in rapid succession. An interview with one of the leading players of Golden Gate United would elevate her status and open her up to more opportunities. "You'd really do that? An exclusive?"

Renzo pushed her eyewear up the slant of her nose with his pointer finger, her gaze going cross-eyed for a second before shifting her focus on him. Her cheeks burned from the simple gesture. "It's the least I can do for the soccer correspondent who believed in me all those years ago and who continues to follow my professional career, even if she is supporting the wrong team."

She huffed a gentle laugh. "I don't know about 'wrong team.' Queen City Royals is in fourth place after playing twenty-six games. It's true they've had more draws than wins, but they've only had four losses. Four! They have a total of forty-two points, which is three more points than Golden Gate United, by the way, so if they keep ..."

Her yammering trailed off when she realized the music had stopped and the space between them had shortened by a few inches. Renzo moistened his lips as his eyebrows pulled down in concentration. She flipped through her mental catalog and identified that expression as the one he wore whenever an opening for a goal was in his sights. The fact that she was on the receiving end both boggled her mind and left her short-winded. Ruining his player stats, even in a hypothetical sense, was not an option. Rella wanted him to go for the goal. She craned forward ever so slightly and tugged down on his jacket's collar.

Darlene, on the contrary, had different plans. She awoke from her nap, the jostle knocking Rella straight into Renzo's chest, his citrus-infused aroma engulfing her. After a few shaky bumps, the elevator began descending at a normal pace.

Renzo's strong hands stroked her arms. "You okay?"

No, because Darlene has the worst timing. Rella nodded, extracted herself from his cozy embrace, and stepped away to retrieve her bag. "Thanks for the dance."

Lorenzo crouched down to grab the autographed clipping, the additional bit of information she included beside her name sparking one of his radiant smiles. "Thanks for the phone number."

She touched her scorched cheeks with the back of her hand, certain the pink splotches were permanently tattooed on her face.

As the countdown to the first floor ticked by, her phone buzzed. She dug it out from her purse and tapped the screen to find the message "Heya Rella" waiting for her from a number she didn't recognize. Her attention snapped over to Renzo, his head slanted down at his own device, but his eyes fixed on her. The line of communication between them was officially open.

Even with his contact on her phone, she felt the need to rewind and confirm she hadn't imagined the last few minutes with him. "Were you serious about the interview?"

"Were you serious about wanting to kiss me?" He was quick on the draw, but she understood why. She wasn't trying to seduce him for her own professional gain. She also didn't care about his money or fame; she just wanted him.

"Ever since high school, so interview or no interview," she started and mustered all of her confidence, "I still want to kiss you. If you're still interested?"

"I am," he said, the corners of his lips twitching into a pleased grin. "And I was serious about the interview. Give me a time and a place, and I'll be there."

Her smile widened as a certain fluff piece raced to the forefront of her mind. "I know a great barbecue spot."

FAR, FAR AWAY

Abigail F. Taylor

I N MARCH OF 2003, The Irish Rangers are deployed to Iraq
in support of Operation TELIC and Iraqi Freedom. By May,
newly appointed captain, Theo O'Connor, has fallen in love.

... It begins with a whisper of hot, fried dough pulsing through
the warm summer air. He's in his street clothes, sunburnt at his
ears, across his high cheekbones, and prominent nose. The
afternoon adhan has finished and the streets swell with foot traffic
and trucks moving too fast around narrow corners, like dusty
gondoliers. People shout out to him, pointing at his big and blond
frame, 'American!' thinking he has more money than he does. But
he knows how to haggle and is fluent in Arabic, even if his tight,
nasal accent occasionally bounces on the wrong consonant.

The reason Theo joined the army in the first place was for
the golden promise of traveling the world. He wishes his
friends were with him now, but most of his battalion is back at
base, hanging out with the marines they've been assigned to
assist. Poor country boy that he is, why would he hang around
the bunkers for endless games of poker when the opportunity

of new experiences was just beyond the gates? Theo liked Baghdad. The people, the architecture, the culmination of spices, warm bread, and stagnant air that is common in all densely populated cities. His only regret is that he arrived not as an individual but as a dangerous cog in an unruly machine.

He walks through Al Bataween without any other purpose but to absorb. The amalgamation of all religions is couched here. Young men and women hang out the shuttered windows of their second and third floor apartments. Or they stand on wrought iron balconies, smoking. Merchants occupy the ground levels, sweeping away the debris of last night's bombings. The destruction is as familiar as a yawn and the old neighborhood still charms through its crumbling despair.

It's fresh zalabia that Theo smells, twinning with slow roasted coffee. He follows it to the cafe at the corner and steps into the cool interior. It is a small place, narrow in the wrong spots with paint peeled double doors that lead to a courtyard where there is better, more cheerful seating. Inside, the divans are white, tufted gold, and so low to the ground patrons might as well be sitting on the pristine floors. There are men drinking tea and behind an ornate, bamboo partition, a place for women. Theo can hear them laughing, and catches snatches of the stories they swap.

Behind the counter a middle-aged woman stands with a notebook, tallying the items on the shelves. Her black khimar drapes across slender shoulders. Beneath it, a blue butterfly cut dress compliments the springs of hazel in her deep-set eyes.

"Hello," she says in English, her voice is a rumble of whiskey, and the back of Theo's knees feel weak.

"Hello," he says in Arabic, and she smiles at him.

"What would you like?"

He orders saffron zalabia and a coffee, which she tells him is double roasted and enriched with cardamon. He nods, too shy to look at her. Her features are wide, arresting, and there is a freckle on the supple curve of her lower lip. He makes a point of putting the exact change on the counter, to not touch her hands as she passes him plate, cup, and saucer.

"By the way," her laugh is just as deep, as potent as the coffee she serves. "Your Arabic is too formal. Too Egyptian."

"I'll remember that," he says.

"It doesn't matter," she tells him. "I just thought you should know there is a difference."

There's an ashtray at the table he chooses, so he pulls out a pack of cheroots and lingers in the first deep drag of nicotine. Theo has a rule about not smoking while on the job and he has kept to it until now. It's been a difficult Spring and he's had trouble compartmentalizing. He tells himself he doesn't feel guilty for the work he does, but still, the cigar is needed.

He lets it dangle loose between his thin lips and flicks through an abandoned newspaper, finding it easier to read Arabic than English. If only he'd known this trick as a child, he might not have dropped out of school and joined the army. When his cigar is at its nub, he reaches for the fried dough. The saffron cuts through his smoke scarred tongue. Stunned by the texture and taste of it, he glances up, planning to ask the woman if she made the pastry herself, and finds that she is watching him suck the syrup from his fingers. Theo blushes. The deep hunger in him shifts and he knows that she is hungry, too.

When he stands to leave, she hands him naan wrapped in paper. It's fresh from the oven, with brown moon-like craters where the oil has pooled, and is too hot to eat. She doesn't wait for him to scramble for money. She simply takes his dirty plates into a back room and shouts to the small boy, who must be her son, sitting on the stairs to hurry with his chores. The boy eyes Theo with suspicion. He slides his Hot Wheels firebird back into his pocket, as though worried Theo would try and steal it from him.

Outside the breeze is dying and there are more motorcycles now, more children in the streets playing football or marbles, or a number of make-believe games where the rules slide on a scale of how fair the majority votes. A few children run up to him, stick their hands in his pockets, and ask for candy. He knows better than to keep his wallet where it's easy to reach, but sometimes he leaves coins there or jaw breakers and sticky taffies because it's important for kids to feel like they've one-upped an adult. There is too much authority in life to not let them win some of the time.

Theo finds a shady spot to sit down and eat the naan. It's warm and buttery, falling open easily inside of his mouth, kissing his throat with seasoned steam. The paper the woman used to wrap it in has writing all over it. Instructions smudged from the heat and grease.

Come back at sundown. My children will be sleeping.

A burnt spot of naan drags down when he swallows hard. At twenty-three, he's never been with a woman, and never thought it might be an issue until now. Surely, she would want a man of certain skill? He could not show, of course. He's supposed to be back at base in time for early morning meetings. Still, the look that passed between them ... the way he *wanted* in a way he had never before. Desire was not a strong enough word.

And yet ...

And yet ...

Theo's afternoon dwindles with indecision. He walks around awhile, ducking into the cinema to watch a movie, tries to email his family in a shoddy internet cafe with exposed wires hanging from the ceiling. In the end, he is a good soldier and knows how to listen to instruction.

Al Bataween is different at night. Lonesome and on guard. No one stands beyond the safety of their walls. No one plays in the street. He can hear the blaring of several televisions, shouts deep in the bellies of these houses, as families cheer for whatever team is playing. Stray cats slink around pot bellied rubbish bins and there is a dog shuffling around the cafe, searching for sweet or savory scraps.

Gold light streams through the lower shutters and one of the doors is held open by a craggy rock. He steps in, ducking his head to keep from smacking it against the frame. The woman is sitting on a stool at the counter, smoking a slim cigarette. Her long lashes flutter when his shadow fills the door.

"What's your name, soldier?" she asks. She hasn't spoken any English to him since that first greeting hours before. He likes how she rolls her Rs.

"Theo. What's yours?"

"Naglaa. Would you like something to eat? To drink?"

"I don't want to put you out, so." He thinks if he were wearing a hat, it would be spinning nervously in his hands.

"It's no trouble. I have leftovers." She offers him dolma and biryani. While he eats, she closes the door, pulls the latch tight, and lights another cigarette. "We sleep downstairs in the basement when it gets too hot but there are nice, quiet beds upstairs. You shouldn't walk around at night. Not with hair like that. Do you like music?"

"Sure, who doesn't?"

"I have some upstairs. Let me show you."

Naglaa uses both of her hands to capture one of his and they sneak up the stone steps to the apartment above the cafe. She has an impressive record collection and stacks of cassettes that are alphabetized on a low bookshelf. The air smells strongly of hashish and she offers him a joint from a vintage cigarette purse that is on the shelf next to ABBA's *Arrival.*

"Mrs. Robinson are you trying to seduce me?" he quotes and she eases him onto a green divan with a little laugh that dances in her hazel eyes.

"That's such a sad movie."

"Och, but the middle part is great."

"Then let's stay in the middle."

Theo thinks she might kiss him now but Naglaa shifts away from him, returns to her music collection and shifts through the albums until she takes out Dusty Springfield. Her movements are measured and calm. Her fingers glide across the arm and she is careful to drop the needle into the liquorish grooves. Theo watches, the shape of her flirting against the loose fabric of her clothes. He's too tall for the divan and attempts to shift his knees in a way that he would look attractive, masculine, and not the awkward school boy that he feels like.

"I haven't been with a man since my husband died," Naglaa tells him.

"That's okay," admits Theo. "I've never been with a woman."

She nods and passes him the lit joint. He inhales, holding the smoke inside of him, while she begins to unpin her khimar. The erotic reveal of her dark, corkscrew hair, shoves Theo to his feet. He closes the short gap between them and the fabric pools around them. Naglaa is staring up at him, her square jaw set defiant, imploring. Their nervous breaths catch between their bodies.

He asks, "Can I touch you there?"

Naglaa nods and guides him through her hair, down to the suddenly exposed shoulder.

"Can I kiss you there?"

"I wish you would."

Theo lowers his mouth to her collarbone and slides his lips down to the swooping bowl of her neck. He traces her throat with soft kisses back to the curve of her jaw, nibbles her ear.

"I like that," she tells him.

And tells him.

And tells him.

An hour passes and he is still exploring her bare skin with his mouth and fingers, which she has licked in equal measure as though she is trying to take back all the saffron and syrup she's fed him. He is naked, too. She takes her turn looking at him, touching him, the scars and ridges, the freckles that dust across his shoulders and broad back, the swirls of chest hair. They've decided there is no need to go all the way, that whatever this is between them needs to be unwrapped slowly and worshiped.

Together they lay on top of her bed, ankles entwined and Naglaa draws circles in his back. He asks about her childhood in Egypt, the reasons her father moved them back to Baghdad. He asks about her sons and her husband. He asks if she likes owning a business. He asks to kiss her again.

In turn, she dissects his own history. What is it like to be the youngest of six? How did his parents keep their family strong when the bombings were at their worst where he was from. She tells him she remembers reading about The Troubles. She says that's why she likes him because they can share each others' trauma without saying a single word. She asks if he likes being a soldier. She asks if she can touch his penis and she shows him how to touch her, too.

Eventually, Dusty Springfield's "Tonight the light of love is in your eyes, but will you love me tomorrow?" fades away to "Allahu Akbar! Ashhadu an la ilaha illa Allah."

And for the first time Theo agrees. *Praise God.*

His hand is on the curve of Naglaa's thigh and he is dazzled by the way her hair fans out on the pillow, silver strands like precious metal framing the face of a long forgotten deity. She rolls onto her side and gazes at him through sleepy eyes. "It's been a long day and you should be going."

Theo kisses her fully, the heat of her tongue pulling him forward until she is on her back. Her work tough hands grab his chest. Holding his hips with her knees, she laughs, "I've trapped the giant!"

"Ireland is made of giants," he tells her, quite seriously. "A giant separated us from all of Scotland. His footsteps tore up the entire Northern shore."

"Do your giants grant wishes?"

"They might do."

"Then I wish to be kissed again."

Theo balances on his heavy forearms, his fingers tracing the thick curls that have spun away from her temples. He presses his big nose to her big nose, nuzzling, probing, before letting his tongue dart into her parted lips.

An eon passes in mere seconds. A minute at best and the adhan finishes. Naglaa slowly tilts her face away. Her gaze travels through the slats of her window. "Back to the real world."

"I'll come back," he promises her.

"We'll see."

Upon his return to base, Theo gets a light reprimand from the guards on gate duty. He's made it back before the mess hall has opened, so it really is a non-issue. Theo is not one of the captains who is a stoic mystery but he does follow the rules and this will give all his friends, and all the Americans, something to talk about. Which makes him nervous. Not about losing his job, no, but about someone discovering the hidden gemstone that is Naglaa. They might take her away from him or, worse, get the wrong impression of who she is as a person.

There is enough time for him to either get coffee, dirty, unflavored, and watery, or change into his uniform before heading to the meeting. He chooses the latter and arrives at the makeshift office on the other side of the compound before the door is bolted shut. War movies never point out the endless meetings and paperwork that is involved in winning a battle. If this were a movie, Theo would already be in his nest, zoning in on some shifty eyed villain. Or, perhaps, he would be that villain. The denial of a mission due to font style and size would be curled in the corner of a cutting room floor.

Theo takes his seat between a male and female marine, both wiping the crust of sleep from their eyes. He doesn't know their names, or that by this time next year, the male will die while he and Theo are stapled together by a twist of shrapnel.

He still feels like he's a grunt trying to figure out the shape of himself in the business of war. Personally, he thinks he lucked into his stripes and promotion because of a shortage in staff. Or maybe how he handled himself during his first tour. Or maybe his skill as a sniper. But he doesn't believe that these two small slivers of his background are enough to tilt the scales.

The meeting revolves around the haboob that ravaged the area in March. Six weeks have passed and the infrastructure of Baghdad remains broken. Today, the petition to fix a mainline pipe has been approved, and the next several hours are spent delegating the protection detail. The job will be six days on and one off.

Theo takes the first shift with twelve others from his battalion and six from the U.S. Marines. The days are long and sizzle the stagnant air. He's never seen a sky so crisp and blue, the way it clashes against the warm red and orange of the earth. He wants to watch the colors shift as the sun migrates over them but keeps his focus on the horizon instead. The only interest he needs to have is in the occasional suspicious glints of what might be metal. What might be a mirage.

Beside him, McCarthy says, "This place is the linchpin of society."

"I thought that was India," says Theo.

"No. That's the linchpin of religion."

"The Bible says that the garden of Eden rests between the Tigris and Euphradis," says Hernandez. "This is where God walked."

"We fucked it up, sure enough, if this is Eden," says McCarthy around a freshly lit cigarette.

Hernandez shakes his head. "You're catholic, O'Connor. You get it."

Theo says nothing. There is already too much weight on him being catholic and enlisting in the ARW, but he thinks that if Naglaa's legs are sacred rivers, then the apex of her is the paradise he will return to.

She is, in fact, surprised to see him when he arrives just as the cafe is about to close. This time, her khimar is a soft pearl color, her dress burgundy and tattered at the hemline, where it collects the dust and heat of the day.

"Are you hungry?"

"Always."

She makes a fresh pot of cardamom coffee and brings out almond croissants. "I'm pretending I'm in France on holiday."

"Outside is the Seine and there is a houseboat waiting for us. We'll take it from Le Harve to Paris and we'll live under the lights of the Eiffel Tower."

"Oh! You speak French!" Naglaa says, delighted, though her eyes remain soft with some unspoken sorrow. She switches languages, too. "Not the Eiffel. It's no prettier than a radio tower."

"Where then?" Theo asks.

She shrugs and moves around the small cafe, sweeping, closing the doors and windows. "Anywhere but here. I'm glad you came. I sent my children to be with my husband's family. It's safer for them."

"Would you want to leave?" asks Theo. He has enough good standing that he can arrange the paperwork. "Back to Egypt where your mother's from or France? Germany?"

Would she want to live in Ireland, cold and wet and beautiful?

Naglaa shakes her head. "You don't leave the place you love just because things get difficult. You stay and fight to fix it."

She leads him up the stairs. This time they listen to Fleetwood Mac and go all the way. Theo is careful when he changes the bedding for her while she is in the bath cleaning up and she returns, dabbing her hair with an old towel. She tells him to bathe while the water is still warm because he smells like her and like gun grease. Once settled back into bed,

Naglaa folds herself into Theo and she gently kisses the calluses on his palms, slides them over her bare breasts.

"I miss being held like this," she says in French.

"What happened to your husband?" he asks in Arabic.

She hesitates, toys with his knuckles that are resting against her nipples. Then she speaks into the empty space of the room. "You people killed him. Or I guess the Americans. He was driving a grocery truck to the border."

"I'm sorry."

She sighs. "It's just how it is. You know this."

"Still. I'm sorry."

"I'm sorry, too."

He tells her about the conversation he had out by the pipeline, his touch tracing from her breasts to her thigh and she rolls over to face him. She holds his head steady, stealing his attention and smooths away the weatherbeaten features. She reminds Theo that not everyone is glad for the western assistance.

"What can I do about that? I have a job, so I do."

"You can go home," she suggests. "Back to your giants and we could have our own strong young men fix the pipes."

He nods. That's true enough but it hurts him that Naglaa both tugs him to her and pushes him away in equal measure. He wonders if she would go with him. Would he mind at all if she used this erupting infatuation to her advantage instead of mutual reciprocation?

Again, Theo stays the night. Is this moving too fast? He wants to know but she is setting the pace. So it isn't. Not for her. He feels wild and numb in his inexperience. He tumbles through this relationship the way a kayaker noses into the foaming white waves and shattering rocks.

He doesn't see Naglaa again for three months. It's not intentional but an ambush happened further north. Saddam's sons are killed in Mosul and half the battalion migrates to assist. Theo loses two soldiers and is sent home to offer condolences to the families. For his own trouble, he is awarded a medal and vacation. Murroe, Limerick is too quiet and carries a green warmth that he's grown unaccustomed to. He keeps to his routine. With endless amounts of free time, he goes to the gym, helps his parents at their pub, and sends long, embarrassing letters to Naglaa. She, in her turn, sends him letters back. Pages that drip in her beautiful script, smudged from the way she grips a pen.

Theo returns to the desert days before the UN headquarters is bombed. He feels at home, strolling down the seats of Al Bataween, smiling to a few familiar faces that smile back. It's the middle of the day, just after the midday adhan. He stays in his preferred chair, sipping the heady coffee while Naglaa serves other patrons, chats with the teens she employs to bake the pastries and clean the dishes. When it seems no one is looking, Naglaa and Theo undress each other with their eyes. She dabs the filtered end of her cigarette suggestively against her lips.

When they're alone again, Theo meets her in the back storage, and they become tangled in the reunion. They are naked on the burlap sacks of coffee beans, holding each other, lazy and satisfied as house cats. Theo probes for the future. He wants what he wants and doesn't mind that she is so much older than him. Does she match him? Is there something he can do to compromise to suit her own needs? Naglaa is careful to avoid talk of weeks and months, potentially years, that are not promised to either of them.

"You're so beautiful," he says and she straddles him, pinning him to the burlap, hair draping over one side of her face.

"Tell me again. How would a poet say it?"

Theo swallows, anxious of sounding stupid or not being impressive enough. One of Naglaa's hands slides to his sternum and her almond shaped nails dance through his chest hair in a way that makes him squirm because it tickles.

Delight bounces in Naglaa's eyes as she threatens him, "I will make you speak!"

"I think if I had the words I wouldn't love you enough," he admits. He has never met a woman so confident of her body or placement in the world. He admires her, is drawn into her, enamored.

One of Naglaa's eyebrows arches. "Love?"

He sits up on his elbows and reaches forward with his mouth, eager to kiss her. His lips land on the curve of her throat. "You don't have to say it back."

"Then I won't," and she makes him forget to fumble for the words he didn't have to begin with.

The UN bombing keeps them separate. Each day he imagines walking down that street to find the cafe empty and gutted by looters. Sometimes, Theo thinks it would be a relief, that Naglaa saw her beloved city crumbling beyond repair and followed her sons to a safer place. After all, when a plane is crashing, the instructions say to put your own mask on first before helping someone else.

How can she and all the other civilians save their home if they're dead? He worries and he worries and he worries and she does not answer his texts. Finally, he is able to leave all the hornet nests his battalion is sent to and heads to Naglaa's cafe with steely determination.

The street is much quieter. More shops are boarded shut with plywood or trash bags. The pavement is cracked from the scraps of metal that fall from the sky, and the feral animals tuck themselves deeper in the shadows, so as not to be seen.

Naglaa and her cafe remain. Theo, still wearing his dusty fatigues, steps in.

There are people he recognizes, who frequent this place as though it is their second home. It certainly is for Theo. When he sees Naglaa coming out from the back with a tray of fresh naan, he almost shouts and rushes to sweep her in his arms and squeeze until she must ask him for air. Her feet stutter in their movements, like her body is willing to play out this tactile fantasy swelling in Theo's throat.

She restrains herself, politely greets him, and returns to her task of putting bread into its display basket. A tiny, pot-bellied man with a white beard and kind eyes, approaches Theo. "Come, let's talk and have tea."

He nudges the small of Theo's back and the two walk into the empty courtyard, sit at a table facing the small wall fountain that once produced a delicate trickle of water. Now it is caked in dust and leaves are captured in abandoned spiderwebs. Naglaa brings out a tea tray and retreats, looking only at the bearded man in an expression that is neither defiant or demure. Simply, Theo realizes, it is resignation.

The man drops two sugar lumps into his cup and drizzles the amber liquid over them. He makes a cup for Theo as well, who drinks it black. He sips and nods. "I don't think it's a good idea for you to hang around here anymore. It gets people nervous."

"It makes you nervous, you," Theo counters. He knows that this man is Naglaa's father. He's seen the old, wrinkled face on her mantle and by the bedside, but he is so very like his daughter. The way they carry themselves, like the Argo or Apollo 11. They have the same clubbed thumbs and steady, deep-set stare.

"It does," the little man agrees. "My daughter is a widow but still has an appropriate reputation in spite of the gossip ... at least you aren't American. So, that's something. All the same, it'll be better if you don't come here. Not in your uniform. Not in street clothes. I think you must be nice or perhaps carry a level of kindness about you that has prevented people from stepping into malicious territory. But please. Stop seeing my daughter."

Theo rubs the stubble around his neck and jaw. "She's a grown woman and capable of deciding what she wants."

"You have a very western view of what you think is best for my daughter. It's not about wants. It's about survival." He raises his hand in surrender and the weight of his words drag Theo's spine down into the center of the earth.

Naglaa interrupts and offers nothing but cautious reprimands under her breath. She demands that her father leaves and when Theo stands, too, she shoves him back into the rickety chair that has given its life to not collapse underneath his weight.

"Stop frightening the customers! If he wants to be overcharged for coffee, let him!" she snaps.

Her father shakes his head, ashamed. Disappointed. Afraid. All of these things that he loops around Theo's neck to hang there like warning signs. This man is a danger. This man rakes his teeth against our soil.

Later, much later, she tells Theo to wear his army boots to bed.

They don't stop seeing each other, though each visit is rarely planned and sporadic as things around them get worse and better and worse again. There are nights where neither undress, but lounge on the divan. He plays with her hair while she reads to him from adventure books. Jules Verne or Tolkein or Brandon Sanderson. Sometimes Theo wiggles the antennae on her television until news and sports channels are able to burst through the heavy lines of static.

The mundane, Theo finds, is an entirely different layer of desire that he is careful not to jostle. He likes it best when he wakes before she does and can make her breakfast in bed. He likes it best when they aren't talking but she is reading, head on his lap, and he is watching the sunrise through her lonely window. He pleads to whatever higher power might be listening to let these quiet moments of intimacy last.

He knows that he is her dirty little secret, that there are so many steps he needs to take in order for Naglaa's community to see him as an honorable man who loves their widow. Still, he says, "I love you."

Naglaa folds her book against her stomach and looks at him. "You're just a boy."

"But I still love you."

"Come back with a ring and we'll see." A smile tugs at the freckle on her lower lip and she returns to her book.

"Alright, so, I will," he says.

Naglaa sets the book aside again and gives him her full attention. She sits up, leans in until they are nose to nose, and Theo can count the velvet loops of her hazel eyes. "Is it a giant's promise?"

"Is that what you wish for?" he asks, cupping her chin in his palm. Before she can answer, he dips her into a kiss. Violent and ugly and precious.

It is said God stopped the sun until a great army avenged itself on its enemies.

Einstein once said that time is only worth what people do with the passing of it.

Theo knows that it stops and starts with Naglaa, that she arrests the day until time slips by them. There is and only ever will be each other.

TWO DOLLS AND A VINYOC

Spencer Koelle

E VELYN CLAY NEVER EXPECTED a handsome woman to fall in her lap. It was lucky for Evelyn that she happened to be seated already, that she was well-padded, and that the woman in question was on the small side.

Evelyn disentangled herself and attained an upright position while her unexpected guest was still spouting language that threatened to peel the skin from her ears.

"Are you alright?"

The stream of words, the mildest of which would have earned her a smack from her father, stopped. The young woman's jaw hung open when her deep green eyes met Evelyn's. Did she have a concussion?

"Sure. I've had worse," the stranger said, shaking her head before dusting off her pinstripe suit. "Nothing hurt except my pride." She swayed. "And maybe my knee."

The red scratches and purple bruising showed sharp against her freckled white skin. She favored her left leg as she bent down, rummaging among the debris before seizing on a squashed lavender trilby.

"Think I can—*ouch*—save it?" the stranger asked, seeming to take the bodily harm in stride.

"Sit down," Evelyn said, forcing her into a chair. "Please," she added. People always said she was too intimidating and forceful. She hoped the moos and crowing had been enough to drown out the sound of the crash.

Evelyn held out a finger, and the beautiful woman's eyes seemed to have no trouble focusing on it.

"Why are you climbing around the side of our barn anyway?"

"I wanted to figure out where smell of good booze was coming from," the woman blurted out, then bit her lip.

"Well then, why didn't you ask?" Evelyn said. She didn't look like a revenuer and the sheriff had already ransacked the place yesterday. "I'll pour you some wine to settle your nerves."

The woman looked at Evelyn like she'd sprouted a second head. "Um, sure, that would be great!" She blinked. "Where are my manners? I'm Sapphire, Sapphire Brooks," she extended a well-manicured hand.

"Evelyn Clay," Evelyn said, taking the dexterous fingers in her calloused grip. "Pleasure to meet you."

• • •

Between the fall and her own unexpected spasm of honesty, Sapphire's pulse was already racing. Miss Clay (no ring) emerged with a wax-sealed coke bottle and two teacups. When she popped the top off, Sapphire's pulse rose up again. The smell promised this was no Motor Engine Schnapps or fruit-flavored paint thinner.

"What brings you out to these parts?" her voluptuous benefactor asked, settling into a twice-repaired sears-roebuck chair with a creak. Her jean overalls were a rainbow of patches straining at the seams, but the button-up shirt had been lovingly tailored to her feminine frame. Sweat glistened on her dark bare arms and cheeks, like the condensation on a drink shaker.

Sapphire hesitated before answering.

34

"Funeral for a business associate," she said, eyes on the repurposed coke bottle. "Name of Guiseppi Vintner."

"My condolences," Miss Clay said. "There's Jon Vintner who works at the mine, but I've never met him."

"We weren't close, but thank you," Sapphire said, hoping that would be enough to forestall any more platitudes. Miss Clay handed her a teacup of wine before pouring her own, and she could tell by the legs it was high-proof. "Aren't you worried I might report you to the police?" she said, careful to gauge the reaction.

"Why would you?" Evelyn asked.

Blackmail, to free up her farm for a rival, or any number of reasons, Sapphire thought. She swished the cup, gave it one more sniff, and then took her first mouthful.

Sapphire forgot to savor it and gasped after she swallowed. This was something she expected from a senator's cellar or a priest's closet. It was dark and rich, with a hint of black cherry and smoke. There was also a strange, almost meaty flavor to it, not bad, but very memorable.

"Thank you," she said, after the screaming of birds and barking of nearby dogs filled the air.

"Least I could do," Miss Clay said, wiping some sweat from her brow and taking a mouthful herself. "You had yourself a nasty shock there." She said absolutely nothing about how Sapphire had brought that shock on herself while trespassing.

Sapphire sipped again, carefully this time. Miss Clay quietly regarded her with eyes the color of whiskey, while the sounds and smells of the farm enveloped her. That round, smiling face had seen more slaps than kisses. Sapphire guessed this lady would be terrible at poker.

"How much do I owe you for the drink?" Sapphire asked, checking that her wallet was still in her trousers.

"Nothing," Miss Clay said, sounding honestly puzzled.

"No, I'm good for it," Sapphire insisted. On top of the drink, this complete stranger had done her a huge favor by not delivering any retribution to her trespassing.

"It's just hospitality!" Miss Clay said.

"At least let me buy you a meal? Your choice of venue," Sapphire said, not saying she would be surprised if this tiny village had more than one hitching post that could be dignified with the name "diner".

"Oh, God Almighty, it's past noon!" Miss Clay said, panic filling her open face. "No, I'm busy for the rest of the day. I shouldn't have lollygagged this long."

"Well, when's the next time you'll be free for a couple hours?"

Miss Clay stared as if there was something in the sentence she didn't understand.

"Tell you what, I'll swing around Sunday evening. I insist," she put her hand on Miss Clay's and felt her shiver. "It's a matter of honor."

•　　•　　•

"But I haven't milked the goats, or checked up on the new grape vines, and the hay—"

Sapphire pressed a finger against Evelyn Clay's lips, then gently pushed her through the doorway.

"Table for two, please," Sapphire said, flagging down a waitress who didn't look overworked.

The waitress, Mabel, led them to a spot near the window, frowning at Sapphire's suit. They must not see many women in navy blue blazers out here in the wilderness of West Virginia.

Sapphire took off her black hat and pulled out a seat for Miss Clay with one practiced motion. She had been easy on the eyes in her farm clothes, but she was utterly stunning in her Sunday best. The faded purple dress hugged her generous figure while obscuring enough to keep things interesting, and the wildflower in her straw hat shone like a gem. Sapphire wrenched her gaze away to the menu. Appreciation was one thing, but she couldn't afford to let a pretty face turn her head again. The steak and eggs couldn't be that good for a dollar fifty, but maybe the soup of the day was worth trying.

"You know, you really could pick any place," she said, struggling to make conversation with those whiskey-colored eyes caressing her suit. "I'm not worried about the price." The half-hour motorcar trip had confirmed that this one-horse town did boast more than a few diners, and most of them looked less cheap than this one.

"I couldn't," Miss Clay laughed. "This is the only one that serves women of my color."

Sapphire sucked in air, trying to draw the thoughtless words back into her lungs. "Oh. I'm sorry."

"Don't be," Miss Clay said, pulling out her fan. "You don't own any of them."

Sapphire would ask around about which clubs were friendly to colored folk before their next date. She should also stop working at the ones that turned out not to be. It was bad business.

"What's good here?" Sapphire asked.

"The cornbread and pinto beans here is the best in town, and the wild mushroom omelet's pretty nice. They've also got a new treat called a Pepperoni Roll, if you're feeling fancy."

Sapphire nodded, holding back that calling anything here "the best in town" was damning with faint praise.

The waitress materialized at her shoulder, either overcoming her distaste for women in men's suits or realizing that the electrum cufflinks indicated a greater capacity for tipping.

"A pot of coffee, two cups, pepperoni roll with cornbread on the side, and whatever madam wants," she said, gesturing at her companion.

"Well, I'll have the mushroom omelet, and uh," she hesitated. "Can I get dessert too? Or a drink?"

Sapphire suppressed a sigh. "Get both." Miss Clay had clearly underestimated her wallet, or was used to people telling her she "didn't need that" when she ate.

"I'll have a glass of lemonade and a slice of pecan pie," she stammered.

When the waitress left, Miss Clay slumped forward, rubbing her forehead. "All that hay needs baling, and I have to bring a casserole to Old Man Tennyson, and the church—"

"Why did you come with me if you were going to worry the whole time?" Sapphire said, trying to control her exasperation. Surely with her wine bootlegging she could afford to hire help.

"Because I promised," Miss Clay said, not taking her head out of her hands.

"I'm surprised you worry about farm chores and community errands, what with your well-stocked cellar," Sapphire said, delicately.

"I don't follow you," Miss Clay said.

While this comely young woman had many good qualities, it appeared that subtlety was not one of them.

"I mean, the cup you shared with me," she said, waggling her eyebrows. "It was exquisite."

"Thank you," Miss Clay said, with an awkward smile.

"I mean," she lowered her voice, "that most shiners can't boast a beverage like that, and a lot of speakeasies would love to get a hold of it."

"Oh, I don't sell it," she said with a hearty chuckle. "Most people who really want booze make their own. Besides, selling alcohol is illegal. I just share it with family and friends."

"So is distilling it," Sapphire said, trying not to pull out her short hair.

"I don't own a still, and I don't put yeast in grape juice or let it spoil," Miss Clay said, with a twinkle in her eye.

Now things were getting interesting.

"And yet you have this delightful drink," Sapphire said. What was her game?

Miss Clay just smiled and folded her hands. Maybe she would be good at poker, after all.

"So, obviously, I'm going to pay for the meal," Sapphire said, "but what do you really want? I'm willing to negotiate."

Miss Clay frowned. "Lemonade, a mushroom omelet, and a slice of pie."

"But you didn't say anything when you caught me trespassing," Sapphire said, fiddling with her blood-red tie, "and you gave me a free drink."

"Yes," Miss Clay said, as if that had settled it.

Sapphire blew out a breath. If she wanted to be enigmatic or cash in the favor at a later date, that was her business. The waitress was coming with their coffee, and it did smell good.

•　　•　　•

"Why don't you ever come over to my place?" Sapphire asked, three months later.

"Well, it's just so hard to get away from the farm," Miss Clay said, smiling. Her words were punctuated with a crack of thunder. "Then when I finish the day's chores, there's all sorts of people around town who need help, and Father's got a bad back, and—"

Sapphire resisted the urge to cover those sensuous lips with her hands, but her expression must have gotten the message across.

"Sorry, I'm rambling," Evelyn Clay said. "I shouldn't complain. Life could be a lot worse for me."

"It could be a lot better too," Sapphire murmured, dealing out the cards. "Seriously, I could pay somebody to take over for the day if it gets you out to my place in Charleston."

Miss Clay almost choked on her gin and tonic.

"You can't do that!"

"Why not?" Sapphire said, putting on her most devilish smile.

"I mean, you can, but you shouldn't!" Evelyn Clay sighed. "You've already done so much for me!"

Evelyn Clay was wearing the ruby broach Sapphire had given her last month, along with the black dress. The copy of *On A Grey Thread* nestled in the basement bookshelf between a volume of Greek poetry and Prose Edda. Either Miss Clay was not inclined towards the pleasures of her own sex, she was very slow at picking up on hints, or she was playing very hard to get.

"Those? Mere tokens of affection," Sapphire said with a dismissive sniff.

Sapphire meant it, too. She knew when clueless men bought her syrupy drinks or silk dresses it wasn't out of the goodness of their hearts, so she should hold herself to the same standards. None of these attempted bribes counted on her side of the ledger.

"I've never had a friend like you," Evelyn Clay giggled.

Sapphire leaned towards the slow-at-picking-up-hints theory.

"Oh really?" she said, in the voice she used to make Gladys Bentley weak at the knees last summer.

"Yeah, you're so nice!" Miss Clay said, punctuating the words with a juicy belch. That set off another fit of giggles, and Sapphire found herself infected by the laughter.

Sapphire wiped her eyes. She couldn't remember the last time she'd used her tear ducts. There had to be some way to get things moving.

She looked at the mismatched low numbers of black and red in her hand.

"How about we make things interesting?"

•   •   •

For some reason, Evelyn was fascinated by the way Sapphire Brooks filled out her dark green blazer and mint button-up shirt. It was strange, the way a men's suit emphasized her firm chest and wide hips. She also had an adorable way of resting her dimpled chin on her hands when she studied her cards.

So far, Evelyn had won nine hands out of eleven. Miss Brooks folded when Evelyn drew a crappy hand. Either she was really lucky, or Sapphire was letting her win.

"You know, what I haven't been able to figure out is," Sapphire said, her voice only slightly slurred, "where are you making all this heavenly nectar? Even if you had a place out in the woods, how would you transport it? This whole land is full of bottle-breaking dirt roads and sudden scary cliffs."

Evelyn pointedly refused to answer the question. It was hard enough trying to figure out if she had a pair of eights or four of a kind. What the heck, she put in the ante anyway and raised by a quarter.

"I hope I'm not imposing by staying here," Sapphire said, rubbing her lips with her thumb.

"I couldn't let you try to drive home in that downpour," Evelyn said, thinking of the government surveyor who died in the mudslide last year. "Anyway, I'm used to sleeping in the barn."

Sapphire sighed. Maybe the bad luck was getting to her. "You know, if I want to buy gas and coffee on the way home, my funds are running low. I really want to keep the game going, though," she said, wiggling her black-stocking-clad feet in the air.

"Don't worry, I know you're good for it," Evelyn said.

"Tell you what, for my wager on the next hand, I'll offer you up a penalty instead of cash." Sapphire twirled her tight orange hair around one finger and sucked the lemon peel from her Bees Knees.

"What would that be?" Evelyn said, feeling strangely nervous. Somehow her glass had emptied. She grabbed one of the wax-sealed coke bottles that contained either old whiskey or new rum and gave herself a refill.

"Oh, sorry! I should have offered you some first," she said, feeling the old fear rise up like spring weeds.

"It's fine, Miss Clay," Sapphire said, waving the worry away. "It's okay to serve yourself first. But back to my original point, I want to wager a favor." She pulled her lips back in a tight, hungry grin, then wiped some sweat from the top of her chest. "I'll do almost anything."

"And what if you win?" Evelyn said, trying to look stern. She might not be as streetwise as her friend, but that didn't mean she'd just fallen off the turnip wagon.

Sapphire blinked and scratched her head, as if the thought hadn't occurred to her.

"Hmm, what could possibly be worth everything I have to offer?" she said, with naked vanity. Her cucumber-colored eyes lit up. "I know!" She hiccuped, then cleared her throat. "You tell me where you get all this top-shelf contraband from!"

"That's a fair trade," Evelyn said. "If I win, then, you'll have to do all my chores for a day, around the house and in the community!" she thumped the card mat with her fist. Sapphire looked strangely disappointed. Too bad. If Evelyn won this, she was going to spend a whole day just reading books and eating bonbons, laying around, while this city slicker got a real taste of hard manual labor.

"Fine," Sapphire said, putting out one smooth little hand. "Shake on it."

"I promise," Evelyn said, sealing the bargain with a squeeze. Sapphire squeezed her hand back even tighter and was very slow to let go.

This time, Evelyn dealt the cards. Sapphire watched her intently, though her eyes rested more on Evelyn's ears and exposed arms than her hands.

"Love the view," Sapphire mumbled.

Evelyn carefully looked at her cards. Queen of Clubs, Jack of Clubs ...

She tried to keep her eyes from going wide or her breath from catching. She took another sip of strong spirits.

Nine of Clubs, Eight of Clubs ... she could feel sweat soaking her hair ... and the Two of Hearts.

She anted up. She really should trade more and hope for a pair, but if she got a straight flush ... there's no way that Sapphire could beat that. Evelyn really wanted to see that snappily-dressed tomboy working the vines, getting all red-faced and sweaty.

"Dealer takes one," she said.

Sapphire locked eyes with her and traded in two cards. "Call."

•   •   •

Evelyn Clay woke up to the sight of an exploding sun, the taste of boiled rat poison, the smell of sick curdled sweat, the sound of something trying to break down her door, and the sensation of pigs fighting inside her skull.

She was surprised, then, to find herself tucked into her own sweet bed with a pitcher of water beside her, instead of in a sticky puddle on the cold ground.

Evelyn realized that the battering noise was actually the regular scrabble of squirrels on the roof. The pigs fighting inside her skull were very large, and the sun still seemed to be busy exploding.

"First hangover?" Sapphire whispered, offering her a fizzing mug.

"How ... what did ..." she winced at the sound of her own voice.

"I dragged you up. Drink this first. Bitters and soda braces your stomach for the next cure. Good thing you keep chickens here."

Evelyn took one tentative sip and realized how thirsty she was.

"Take it easy, slowly, there you go," Sapphire said, gently tilting the glass.

Nobody had taken care of her like this since ... well since her second brother was born. If she got sick, she just had to sweat it out and fend for herself. Of course, when mom and dad got hung over on Evelyn's gin everyone in the house needed to tiptoe around them.

"Alright, now we'll give that a few minutes to settle. Do you remember the game last night?"

"It was ... poker?" Evelyn rasped. "You lost some money, then ... no, I won the first three rounds and you won a round ..."

Sapphire sat there, tapping her foot with a thoughtful look on her face.

"You promised me the secret of your marvelous elixirs," Sapphire said, expectantly.

"Did you win?"

"Yes," Sapphire said, voice level and face neutral.

Evelyn sighed, too loudly, and clutched her head.

"Here, knock this back in one gulp," Sapphire said, handing her a teacup with something glutinous in it. It smelled salty and spicy and faintly of breakfast.

"To your health," Evelyn said, and downed the mixture without hesitation.

The horrible oily texture hit first, then the bitterness and spice, then the pain as the intensity rose.

"Jesus Christ the Savior, what was that?" Evelyn said with a full-body shudder.

"Prairie oyster. It's a kill-or-cure, but I bet your mouth doesn't taste like bile anymore."

Evelyn was too busy coughing to say that it tasted worse. Her stomach lurched twice but accepted the horrible load, and within moments she really felt better.

"You know, I'm not going to hold you to that promise," Sapphire said. "You were totally wasted."

"I gave you my word," Evelyn said, as firmly as she could. "And you were drunk too."

"Okay," Sapphire said, looking out the window. "So what's the secret?"

Evelyn wiped the back of her mouth.

"Follow me."

• • •

Pine needles and twigs crunched underfoot. Some lonely creature screamed overhead. The mist rose out of the ground and spilled down from the mountaintop. The air smelled rich, green, and old.

"There, we should be out of sight from the farm now," Evelyn Clay said, looking around and rubbing her hands together.

The morning chill penetrated Sapphire's suit like bullets. The sun was lost in the canopy, and every direction looked pretty much the same.

"Seems like a good place to dump a body," Sapphire said, with a jolliness she didn't feel. "Hope I'm not about to get murdered."

Miss Clay looked shocked. "I would never do anything to hurt *you!*"

"Sorry, just a bad taste joke," Sapphire said, only half truthful.

She didn't see any wooden shack or metal tubing. There wasn't a shallow cave or wayward pine to hide jugs. Was she going to open up a trapdoor in the solid rock?

Evelyn Clay knelt, closed her eyes, and began to sing. The words were in some foreign language, but deep and rich, so that they sounded like a chorus echoing off the stone heights, mingling with the song of hidden streams and wild beasts. Was it some kind of signal?

A long, low cry answered the song, something mournful as a blues singer dying of an overdose, yet sweeter than grenadine syrup. It also sounded very, very big.

Crunching gave way to thumping and the sound of hooves on stone, but all wrong for a horse, or a goat, almost like an entire herd of animals. Was she going to be trampled to death by wild bison or whatever lived out here?

The mist dissolved. The thing that bounded forward was almost like a deer, but longer, more graceful, and at least twice the size. It moved wrong. Its face was wrong.

Eventually, torn between intoxicating wonder and knee-knocking terror, Sapphire figured out why it was moving so strangely. It walked on six legs. It took longer to notice that because she was focusing on its four glowing purple eyes.

Evelyn whistled the tune, gave her a smile of infinite smugness, and lifted up her hand to the monster. It gently butted it's nose against her head, then thumped one leg on the ground impatiently. It looked hungry.

Unconcerned, Evelyn lifted up a handful of sugar cubes. It reached out a long, forked tongue and plucked them from her hand with the tenderness of a nanny. The creature chewed contentedly, as if savoring the treat.

"What in the God-Damned ... what the Hell ... what is that?" Sapphire sputtered.

"It's a vinyoc. Well, that's what I call them anyway. It's also where I get all my special drinks."

Sapphire blinked.

"Did you, like, breed it? Tame it?"

Evelyn laughed like a brook. "No, I just sing and she comes." She reached up and scratched its chin. The creature leaned into the gesture and regarded Sapphire with four wary phosphorescent eyes.

"They go after grapes mostly, and then you milk it to get wine. I realized it's udder gives gin if you feed it juniper berries, sugar for rum, elderberries for elderberry wine. Getting the mix for whiskey is tricky, because if I don't get it just right it just comes out as rather weak beer, and I haven't figured out how to get brandy yet."

Sapphire decided to close her mouth before something flew in it.

•　　　•　　　•

"You're sitting on a gold mine here!" Sapphire whisper-shouted. "Or a copper mine at least. Think about it. Made-to-order supplies ready in hours instead of weeks or days! High-quality liquor that transports itself!"

"Well, milking an animal definitely isn't illegal, but selling alcohol is," Evelyn said. "Anyway I didn't want to risk getting caught. I just want to make an honest dime." She tried to focus on the beautiful dancers on the stage. Men liked to see women showing off silk and skin, of course, but it surprised Evelyn to learn that Sapphire was also a regular here.

"Look, there's two ways to get rich," Sapphire said, as a wide-hipped white woman in black lace took center stage. "You can get born with money, or you can get rich by crime. There's some people who say there's a third way involving hard work, but they're usually people who got rich by Method One hoping you won't take their money with Method Two." She cracked open a peanut as if exposing the hypocrisy.

Evelyn wanted to point out the problems with this reasoning. There were lots of ways to make money, although most of them involved already having money to spend, and of course somebody like her would be laughed out of a bank if she asked for a loan ...

The girl on stage peeled off her glove with the assistance of a leggy blonde in red, who kissed it before flinging it into the audience. The backup dancers mimed shock and swooning.

"We could be partners, you know," Sapphire said. She drummed her left fingers on the booth while her right hand inched closer to Evelyn's leg.

"Business partners?" Evelyn asked, not sure why her voice sounded so uncertain. She popped a handful of raisins into her mouth to cover her awkwardness.

"Sure," Sapphire said. "Business partners." Her hands froze, and there was a strange bitterness in her words. The charming redhead shook herself. "I was thinking fifty-fifty?"

"Sounds good," Evelyn said, and Sapphire almost choked on her peanuts. "I mean, if you think that's fair."

"*You're* asking *me* if it's fair?" Sapphire wheezed, thumping her chest. "Sweetheart, I've got connections, bartending skills, and specialist knowledge of the trade, but you're still the one with the vinyoc. You've got all the power here. Aren't you even going to haggle?"

Evelyn leaned in close, close enough she could count the freckles on Sapphire's neck, and whispered "I trust you."

Sapphire jerked back so hard she almost fell out of her seat. She laughed nervously.

"Honey, don't trust anyone."

She didn't fool Evelyn. This was somebody who really needed a friend.

"That's if we go ahead with it," Evelyn said. "I'm still uneasy about the whole prohibition thing."

Sapphire put a tender hand on her shoulder.

"And just when is the last time you did something for yourself? Not because somebody asked you to, or because it needed to be done, or because it was expected?"

•   •   •

"Let me help you with that," Sapphire said, grabbing the sweet vermouth.

"It's okay, I've got it," Evelyn smiled, picking up the John Bartram's specialty bitters.

Evelyn was wearing the amethyst broach Sapphire had gotten her last week, over a reddish-purple dress she'd picked up with some of the proceeds from the previous month's operation in the abandoned mine. That was a good sign. There was no way to tell if she'd read the book of poetry, though.

Thin Tony watched the shaker with cold, focused eyes. The poison ivy and wild grapevines covering the abandoned church cast him into piebald shadows. His favor could mean a lot for their enterprise. Maybe she should have insisted on mixing the Manhattan herself.

"Best of this month's harvest," Evelyn said, as she garnished the drink with a luscious cherry.

Tony Kotchever eyed the drink critically, sniffed it, then took a sip. The cynicism left his eyes. The lines of his hard face softened as he exhaled, and he took another sip, slower this time.

"Thank you, Ma'am," he said, in a heartfelt voice. He tipped his hat, picked up the drink, and left for the swept stones they'd turned into a dance floor.

"You sure impressed him," Sapphire said, making sure she sounded calm. "I guess now that you can mix Manhattans, you don't need me anymore," she joked.

Evelyn turned to her, the sunlight winking off her broach. "Why would I do that?"

Sapphire opened her mouth to explain it was a bad joke, but the mayor swaggered up to the propped-up planks and barrels demanding Evelyn's attention. Sapphire sighed and went to the other end of the makeshift bar.

When the Pastor's wife asked for a Paris Side Car, Sapphire kept up pleasant conversation while shaking the mixer so hard it almost flew out of her hands.

They'd been at this gig for a while, and they had to give Thin Tony his cut. Maybe it was time for her to cash in, pick up stakes, and move back to the city. It wasn't like things here were going to go anywhere.

A pair of light brown hands stopped Sapphire when she attempted to make a sloe gin fizz with dark rum. The hands were attached to a plump young man she'd seen around town, with long lashes and bright violet eyes. A few leaves were stuck in his hair, but he was otherwise as immaculately dressed as the best female impersonators.

"I think I can handle this one," Dennis, that was his name, said. "Here, you have this and go relax."

Sapphire bit back a withering profane insult, took a breath, and handed him the seltzer bottle. "You're right." She raised the copper mug to her lips. It was gingery, sour, and sharp with something she couldn't recognize.

"What is this anyway?" she asked when he finished serving the town doctor.

"Twenty years early," he mumbled.

Sapphire shrugged and headed for a folding chair. Everyone had their secrets.

"Sorry about that," Evelyn said, coming over with her glass of Chardonnay in one hand and a familiar-smelling cocktail in the other. "Mayor Whiteman does ramble on, and I couldn't get away. I thought you could use some refreshment. Luckily, Dennis Semele intervened. I wonder who invited him."

Sapphire tasted the drink and moaned with delight. "A Bee's Knees, with blueberry honey! My favorite." She smacked her lips. "I could get down on my knees and kiss you."

"What do you mean?" Evelyn said. "Of course I got your favorite."

Sapphire sighed and downed both beverages.

"Never mind."

•   •   •

Sapphire raised her electric light and peered into the narrow cave. There was no crate of straw with twelve pints of gin and a concealing layer of farm-fresh eggs. Instead there were two jugs of bubbly rose-gold, and a small pile of wrapped gifts.

"This isn't enough for Fiorenza Kotchever's wedding," Sapphire shouted to nobody.

"I already filled that order," Evelyn said, causing Sapphire to jump so high she banged her head on the cave.

"Holy shit! Don't sneak up on me like that!"

"I'm sorry!" Evelyn said, quickly putting a hand to her head. "Do you need ice?"

"I'll be fine," Sapphire said, waving her off. "What is this?"

Evelyn's frown turned back into a broad smile. "It's champagne, just for us." She gestured at the packages. "And I got these for you."

Sapphire frowned. "But, it's not my birthday or Christmas. And I didn't bring anything for you. Why would you do this?"

Evelyn stifled a laugh and shook her head. "Just open them."

Sapphire's hands shook and an unfamiliar tightness clutched her chest. She handled the lilac-wrapped packages as if they might be nitroglycerin.

The first one contained a pair of perfectly-fitting duck egg blue mittens. Then there was a jar with a note explaining it was the last of Granny Clay's blackberry preserves. Finally, there was a sealed envelope containing a sheet of music with some kind of foreign poem.

"Thank you, they're wonderful," Sapphire said, still trying to figure out what Evelyn's angle was here, "but what about this?" She held up the paper like a shield over her chest.

"That's the song I sing," Evelyn said. "It calls the vinyoc."

Sapphire staggered back.

"Why ... why would you give me this?" she forced the words out.

"Now you don't need me anymore," Evelyn said, gently.

"Why would you say that?" Sapphire said. She set the mysterious gifts down on the ground before her trembling fingers could drop them.

"You said it first," Evelyn said, still smiling, but with just a little trace of sadness and mockery. "So now, you have to decide if you really don't need me, or if I really don't need you."

Sapphire stared at her, waiting for the next thought to arrive.

"You must have thought I was a real Dummy Dora," Evelyn said. "But I was reading over the poetry of Sappho, and I finally figured it out."

She took a step forward. Sapphire wanted to step forward and wanted to run off like a startled deer.

"Do you love me? The way men and women love, I mean?"

Sapphire licked her lips and cleared her throat. She felt like she'd downed three shots of the sharpest room-temperature rotgut.

"I mean, I don't love men the way women love men, and you're sweet, and beautiful, and I—" Sapphire coughed, choking on her spittle.

"Yes or no?" Evelyn said, folding her arms. Her voice was firm, but her eyes glistened.

"God, yes," Sapphire gasped, and the second time that decade she found her tear ducts functioning.

Evelyn pounced on her, expertly knocking them both to the leaf litter and pinning her with her supple softness.

"Then show me," she whispered into Sapphires ear.

The two women writhed together on the ground, whispering poetry and exploring each other's bodies. On the cliff overhead, the vinyoc nursed its fawn.

A PIGEON IN WINTERSET

Perk Perkins

IT WAS A BEAUTIFUL, WARM DAY in April. Spring was in full swing in Winterset Iowa and Anna had all her windows wide open to invite the fresh, warm, cleansing breeze inside. The harsh winter air would be pushed out by force, as spring has much more power and authority than any other season. Spring is the season of brand-new life as well as the rebirth of dormant species.

Winter in Iowa is intense, especially for the trees. In fall their leaves all turn beautiful colors of red, yellow and orange. People come to Winterset from all over the state to enjoy the beauty of the autumn glory, the collage of color and the old-timey covered bridges. The second week of October the town holds the Covered Bridge Festival in the square. Anna and many of the ladies in town set up tables to sell their jams, jellies and canned jalapeño peppers. There is a contest held for every known fruit or vegetable that can possibly be canned or pickled. The winners go on to sell out of their fine product and for an entire year they are considered a minor celebrity in town. Jalapeños are the most popular pickled item in all of Madison Country and Anna had won the blue ribbon for her jalapeños the last two years.

Anna was in her mid-forties with an hour-glass figure, but the sand had shifted a bit over the years. She always had a pretty face and a Colgate smile, and along with her two blue ribbons it raised the ire of a few of the local old maids. Many looked up to her, but some of the wrinkled spinsters, the ones with few prospects for a happily-ever-after, were bitter and spread lies about her jalapeños being store bought at the Hy-Vee. In Winterset Iowa, that's a horrible thing to say about a woman. Why it was the same as using the F-word. But that's your reward for living in such a peaceful, charming town and Anna accepted it.

Soon after the festival, Old Man Winter blows into the state and inhumanely strips the trees of their beautiful plumage. Now, they must stand in the cold and snow, naked and embarrassed for month after month. The oaks, maples, walnut and cottonwood trees pray for an early spring, while the pines, holding all their needles year-round, simply smirk and act arrogant.

But now the trees were all budding and the wildlife was busy procreating and Anna's house was a fresh smelling, happy place. Even Elvis, the green parakeet, was whistling extra loud and bright, possibly hoping to attract the attention of some love-starved wild sparrow who was a nonracist and had an open mind. Or perhaps a female budgie, on the lamb after escaping its owner, might hear Elvis' beautiful song and rush to his side. But for now, he could only kiss his cuttlebone and admire the dashing, gorgeous green parakeet in the mirror in his cage.

Anna was in the laundry room when she heard Elvis squawking intensely. It was the same alarm she heard when a daddy-long-legs wandered into his cage. That was before he knew they were so delicious. Anna stuck her head out the door and scolded Elvis. "What are you whining about?"

It was then she saw it. Sitting on the window ledge in the kitchen; a pigeon. She smiled and walked slowly to the window. The pigeon was panting wildly and seemed exhausted. "Did you see an open window and want to check it out little birdie?" She cooed to the pigeon. "You look tired. I bet you're thirsty."

She pulled two small, white, ceramic bowls from an upper oak cupboard. She filled one with tap water and set it down in front of the feathered visitor. The pigeon drank ferociously as if it hadn't had a drink in days. "Oh my!" Anna exclaimed. She reached under the sink and got the box of Elvis' budgie food. She poured the seeds in the other bowl and presented it to the pigeon under the scrutiny of Elvis' unapproving glare. The pigeon dove into the bird seed with similar reckless abandon, scattering seeds and husk everywhere.

It was then Anna noticed that the bird had a silver-colored capsule fastened to its left leg. She moved slow, so as not to scare the bird, and picked him up and removed the capsule. The pigeon was obviously used to being handled as he didn't protest in the least. The capsule unscrewed to reveal a piece of rolled up paper inside. Like a miniature scroll, she unrolled it and read the message.

'Communication truck destroyed. No radios. Under attack. Launch airstrike, 51.3397 N, 12.3731 E. Only have ammo for two more days max.'

Anna didn't understand what it meant. *Under attack? Airstrike?' It was 1965 and President Johnson had just announced in March that he was sending American troops to Vietnam. 'Surely this pigeon couldn't have flown all the way from southeast Asia?* she thought.

She looked at the weary pigeon and wondered. "I'll call Iverna and see if she has any ideas what's going on." She said to the pigeon.

On the phone Anna explained to her best friend about the pigeon and the note. Iverna's reply was thirty-seconds of laughter. When she finally composed herself, she snorted, "Anna ... c'mon ... you know better."

Perplexed Anna asked, "Know better than what?"

Still giggling Iverna said, "Anna, what is the date today?"

"April 1st, 1965. So?" she replied.

"Right. It's the first day of April ... April Fool's Day. Someone got you good!" The laughter continued.

"Oh Lordy. How can I be so stupid. April Fool's Day. What a dope I am." She laughed at herself. "Well, it's only nine in the morning so I better get ready for a long day of pranks now that folks know I'm so gullible."

"Oh Anna you'll be fine." Iverna assured. "I have to go hang the laundry on the line, I'll talk to you later. Tell Elvis I said hi."

Anna hung-up and smiled at her own ignorance. She walked into the kitchen toward the pigeon that made her a fool. As she walked by his cage she said to Elvis, "Iverna says hi." Elvis chirped.

Anna poured a cup of coffee from the percolator and sat at the yellow Formica topped kitchen table. As she sipped her coffee it struck her. 'I think I'll write back to that smart aleck." She pulled a small notepad from the junk drawer along with a pen and began to write.

'I'm sorry but your pigeon must have missed a turn at Saigon and came to America by mistake. I have no rockets or bombs or whatever you needed. Sorry. But by the way it was a great April Fool's joke.'

She giggled as she rolled it up and stuck it into the capsule. As she fastened it to the pigeon's leg she told it, "Feel free to rest up for the day bird." But as soon as she set him on the windowsill, he took off and flew high into the air. She ran outside to watch him as he went straight up, very high. Then he flew in perfect, wide-ranging circles for a couple minutes before heading east like a rocket.

"Whoa ... he sure looks like he knows where he's going." She chuckled.

The rest of the day Anna kept busy with spring cleaning and listening to the Hi-Fi. Her music taste varied depending on her mood. Today was a mixer with Eddy Arnold, Jim Reeves, Patsy Cline, The Beatles and Fats Domino. As the mellow country songs played, she sat and listened in quiet reverence while she smoked a Kool cigarette on the front porch. The Beatles and Fats always made her dance, which turned her into a much more vigorous and thorough spring cleaner.

At about four-thirty, as she was taking her laundry off the line in the backyard, she saw the pigeon fly by her and into the kitchen window. She hurriedly grabbed her laundry basket and rushed into the house. A couple socks blew off onto the grass, but she left them.

The screen door slammed behind her which startled Elvis but not the pigeon. He had flown right onto the kitchen table and was once again panting. Anna pulled out the two small bowls and quickly filled them with birdseed and water. She took the capsule off his leg and unrolled the message.

'I don't know what's going on there or where Saigon is but this ain't no damn April Fool's joke. You know we're in Leipzig Germany and I sent you the coordinates for the strike. The krauts are closing in … we need an airstrike and troops … soon!'

Now she was sure in her heart, in her soul, that this was no gag. The desperation that she could sense, was real. This was a poor soul trapped in a situation and the light of hope was fading. Where was he? He claims Germany, but there is no war in Germany. And a pigeon surely couldn't travel across the Atlantic Ocean. And even if it could … why would it show up at her house in Winterset Iowa. Twice! Her right hand tried to take a pulse from her left wrist. She quickly gave up when she remembered she had no idea how to take a pulse.

Okay … she thought. *I'll just get straight to the point. There's got to be an explanation and if this is a joke, he is a sick bastard.* She took out the small notepad and wrote …

'Listen, I am not going to play along with your sick joke. My name is Anna and your pigeon landed in MY kitchen in Winterset Iowa. There hasn't been a war in Germany in twenty-years, so I don't why, or how you're asking for help? There are no troops in Germany. This isn't funny anymore, leave me alone.'

"That should do it." She said to Elvis boastfully.

She rolled and placed the message in the capsule and fastened it onto the homing pigeons' leg and placed him on the kitchen windowsill. He instantly took to the air and fluttered out of sight.

As darkness slowly drew the shade on the day Anna made the rounds and closed all the windows in the house. She opened Elvis's cage door as she did every evening. He quickly flew out and lit upon her shoulder, his favorite place in the world.

From his perch he watched her fix a BLT sandwich on the stove and pour a glass of white wine. She sat at the yellow kitchen table and started to nibble at her sandwich. Seeing breadcrumbs scattered about, Elvis flew down to the table and cleared the area around her plate of all crumbs and foreign matter. She rubbed the back of his head with her fingertip, and he tilted his head down for her. His eyes closed in ecstasy, and they shared a loving moment, one of thousands over the years.

"You would never try and trick your mama like that mean person, would you Elvis?" She asked him in baby/parakeet talk.

In a very high pitched, squeaky voice he sung, "You ain't nothing but a hound dog."

She pulled him up to her lips and kissed his beak tenderly. "I love you Elvis." She swooned.

Elvis squawked back, "I love you Cilla."

The next morning Anna awakened with the early morning rays of sun warming her legs under the colorful quilt. It was her favorite way to wake up and usually foretold her day was going to be wonderful. She threw on her shabby, pink robe and went downstairs to plug in the percolator.

As Elvis caught sight of her on the stairs, he began his early morning love chirps. She was just as happy to see him as he was to see her. She put her face up to his cage and greeted him with her baby budgie voice. "How's my little king of rock and roll?"

He chirped at her sweetly with loving eyes. She repeated it again in hopes of getting a human song lyric response, but some days Elvis just wanted to be a parakeet. Today was such a day.

She realized too that this was one of those days, so she pressed on to the kitchen to plug in the coffee pot and put two slices of Wonder Bread in the toaster. She liked her toast setting on five. That's a bit dark and bitter for most people, but she had been a five girl all her life.

She got the butter from the fridge and the cinnamon sugar from the breadbox. She opened the kitchen curtains to check out the windmill in case she needed to wear a hat today. "Ohhh!" she exclaimed. There was the pigeon sitting on the windowsill staring intently into Anna's eyes. "You scared the tar out of me."

She opened the window and the bird quickly fluttered over to the kitchen table, searching for the two familiar bowls. Anna quickly obliged, her breath quickened with excitement, anticipation and a little fear. Once the bowls of food and water were presented, she roughly grabbed the pigeon and removed the capsule. With shaky hands she took out the message, which was much thicker, and read it as she trembled.

'I can scarcely believe what I read. Can this be MY sweet wife, Anna. The love of my life waiting for me in Winterset? Darling I've been sending for help as we are trying to take Leipzig, Germany on our way to Berlin to kill that paper hanging son of a bitch Hitler. But our HQ is only ten miles away and I can't reach them. We need their support desperately. Communications are all down and we only have homing pigeons to rely on. The only answer I have gotten back is from you. I'm so grateful for this miracle but how the hell is it possible? I love you sweetheart. The war is almost over, I'll be home soon.'

Anna dropped the small, rolled up message, her eyes rolled back in her head, she fainted and dropped to the pale linoleum floor. Elvis sadly and quietly chirped.

Ten minutes later Anna came to. She slowly sat up, rubbed her eyes and wondered if she was in a dream. She pulled herself up to the table on her knees. She saw the message curled up on the table and knew it hadn't been a dream as she hoped. Somehow, someway, this was real. Her husband Henry, who had been killed in WWII, was now alive and sending her messages from the German battlefield in 1945. It was so impossible, and yet the reality was, it was actually happening.

Her mind reeled a mile a minute. Old memories of her dear husband overwhelmed her and she found it hard to breath. She made it to her wobbly feet and inched her way to the cupboard over the stove. She pulled down a bottle of ten-year-old Johnnie Walker whiskey. She put it to her lips and tipped it high. She lowered the bottle while she grimaced from the burn in her throat and nasal passages. Her eyes glanced at the cuckoo clock over the television. It was only seven in the morning. She raised the bottle again and felt the burn, even embraced the burn ... she needed the burn.

As she put the bottle on the counter the little bird popped out of his miniature wooden chateau and seven times bellowed, cuckoo, cuckoo ... Elvis matched him cuckoo for cuckoo as the small wooden clock bird had been his tutor. From the kitchen she could see into the living room and over the fireplace hung a large portrait from their wedding day. It was her most treasured memory. They were both smiling, both ecstatically happy and that's the memory she kept in her heart all these years.

"I must write him back and tell him how much I love him. My god, it's been so long." She cried aloud.

She had left the pen and pad on the Formica top table, and she wrote frantically.

'My darling husband Henry. To read your words thrilled my heart in ways I thought I would never feel again. I recognize your handwriting from so many of your poems and love letters that I read daily. It really is you. I don't know how it's even possible, but I know it's you and I can feel your love from so far away and somehow over two decades later time has reconnected us. Know this, I love you more than any woman has ever loved any man. And that love will never die. My heart remains yours and yours alone and we will share our hearts one day again in God's glory.'

Anna hurriedly rolled the paper and stuffed it into the cylinder. She fastened it to the pigeon's leg and practically threw him out of the window. She took another long, burning pull off the whiskey bottle as she watched the pigeon wing his way up into the sky and somehow she prayed, to her husband.

The day seemed to drag by slowly for Anna. She needed to make a trip to the grocery store, but she didn't want to chance on missing the pigeon's return. She could get by without bread, toilet paper, eggs, milk and food in general. She wasn't going to miss the pigeon.

Day turned to night and Anna climbed the stairs to her bedroom. She went to her double closet and picked out her husbands' favorite cardigan. From her top clothes drawer she removed Henry's twenty-year-old Zizanie men's cologne. She sprayed just a bit of the woody, warm, spicey fragrance on the sweater and held it to her breast, inhaling him softly and slowly, just like she had done so many nights. She drifted off to sleep with a sweet, warm, contented smile.

At four that morning, as the red glow on the eastern horizon threatened to start another day, Anna's eyes popped open. She sat up and swung her legs out of the high, soft, featherbed. She slid on her furry, pink slippers and then realized she was wearing

Henry's dark green sweater. She didn't remember putting it on in the night, but no matter, it would do wonderfully for her robe this morning.

As she rushed down the stairs preoccupied, she didn't even notice Elvis' quiet, little chirp of, "Love you Cilla." She went to the kitchen window to find it empty. No pigeon and just a crescent of sun was pushing back the Iowa darkness.

She opened the window as high as possible and stuck her head out. No pigeons in sight, but the sweet songs of the early morning robins and meadowlarks decorated the air. Anna filled the percolator up with Maxwell House coffee and plugged it in. The two white, ceramic bowls were filled with budgie seeds and water and placed on the table in front of her. She held her empty coffee cup in her hand as she sat at the table and waited for the coffee pot to do its thing.

Tap, tap, tap, tap ... Anna's eyes slowly fluttered to attention as she raised her tired head from the table. Just then the cuckoo clock began chiming. As if finished its final sixth whistle, the brain fog raised and Anna saw the pigeon inches away, pecking at the seed bowl, having emptied it completely.

"Oh my Lord!" she shouted. She grabbed the pigeon and removed the capsule and then the scroll of paper.

'My sweet, sweet Anna ... I know this is an unnatural situation, and I don't understand any of it. I loved your sweet, tender words and never will they leave my mind or my heart. Your message said that time has reconnected us after two decades? What does that mean sweetheart? Am I not going to make it back home to you? Will I never get to hold your warm, beautiful body in my arms again? The children we longed for ... are they never to be born? The wonderful life we were sharing together, is it truly over? How do you know this my darling?

It's getting very bad here Anna. The Krauts have us surrounded and we're nearly out of ammo. My men are so afraid that they are losing their minds. It's up to me to protect them ... and I will. Please understand how I long for your kisses and pray for the day that somehow, I may taste your lips once more ... taste the sweetness, the honey, the true love that seals every one of your perfect kisses. Henry.'

Anna's eyes rained onto the table and the small sheet of paper soaked up much of it. Her breathing was shallow and erratic with fear and worry. 'I've got to tell him that maybe, just maybe, this miracle will continue. Maybe he will be spared this time and come home to me. I can't let him lose hope.' She thought.

She pulled her pad of paper close and quickly scribbled, 'Don't give up hope my husband. Pray ... pray for a miracle as I am doing. Pray and don't give up hope.'

She rolled up the paper as fast as she could and stuffed it into the cylinder. When she looked up, the pigeon was on the open windowsill. It was staring at her with small, sad eyes and his head was lowering shamefully. Anna knew from that look in its eyes that it must be too late. The miracle was over. The pigeon turned away and regretfully launched himself from the window, his wings pounding the air, rising quickly until he disappeared into a white, fluffy cloud.

She slowly rose and staggered to the window, but he was already gone, his purpose fulfilled, his mission now complete.

She wobbled back to the kitchen chair and staired at the window, her hollow eyes reflected her grieving soul. She sat motionless, tearless, thoughtless for fifteen minutes. Then she went into the closet in the study. She came back to the table with a grey file box. She pulled out a handful of papers and scattered them on the table, searching. Finally, she found it, the envelope she was looking for and pulled out the telegram, reading it slowly.

The United States Army regrets to inform you that your husband, Corporal Henry Lee Kelly, was killed in action the morning of April 3rd, 1945, near Leipzig, Germany.

Anna looked at the calendar on the fridge.

It was April 3rd, 1965.

She glanced at the cuckoo clock; it was six thirty.

Corporal Kelly had received the Purple Heart citation for suffering injury in battle the week before his death, but he refused treatment at a military outpost and refused to leave his men.

The German army nearly surrounded and closed in on the ten remaining soldiers. Corporal Kelly ordered his men to escape through the forest while he held off the advance, giving no thought to his own safety. He killed over thirty enemy soldiers and held them off for an hour, until he ran out of ammunition, allowing his men to escape to safety.

For this incredible act of heroism, he will receive posthumously, the Bronze Star and his commanding officer has submitted needed documents for the highest honor in the military, The Medal of Honor. Your president and a proud nation send it deepest condolences.

Anna reached into the file box and pulled out a large and a small black box. She opened them both and gazed emotionless at the Bronze Star and The Medal of Honor. She slowly shook her head without sentiment.

She pulled the lapel of the cardigan up to her nose. She breathed in several long, deep, soulful breaths causing the birth of a smile to grow on her tear-stained face.

"I love you Cilla." Elvis chirped lovingly.

Anna whispered, "I love you too Elvis.

Feeling groggy from the emotional earthquake she just barely survived, she lay her head in her folded arms on the table and drifted off into a gloomy, coma like rest.

The screen door banged loud in the kitchen and startled both Elvis and Anna. It woke Anna from her stupor and she rubbed her eyes and stared at the blurry vision walking towards her.

"Taking a catnap are we dear?" The familiar voice asked as it came closer.

Anna gasped, almost choked ... she couldn't believe her slowly clearing eyes.

"Henry! Henry ... is it really you?" She exclaimed as she jumped up from her chair and into his arms, full of a joy she had never known before.

Henry laughed and twirled her in his arms. Those arms seemed even stronger than she last felt. She rubbed his curly brown hair that now had wisdom streaks of gray on the sides. He bore a few more wrinkles, fewer than her, but he was as handsome as ever.

"What happened to you? Where have you been all this time?" She cried.

He shook her playfully. "Baby, I just took junior to baseball practice and picked up some rabbit and chicken feed at the co-op. I've only been gone a couple hours. I didn't wanna wake you."

"Junior?" She mouthed. She looked into the living room above the fireplace to see a large portrait of Henry and her and a handsome teenage boy in between them. The boy was the spitting image of Henry and it was the happiest family she'd ever seen.

The table was empty—no file box, no papers, no telegrams, no medals.

"Are you alright Anna?" He asked. "Do you need a doctor or a shot of Johnny Walker?" He half joked.

She kissed him passionately. "I don't need anything darling. I'm just so glad you're finally home."

IRIS IMMORTAL

Jared Kerr

FOR SOME REASON, I'd always believed that vampires kept diaries. You can imagine my disappointment when I discovered I was the only one. The only vampire who kept a diary, I should say, not the only vampire. There are hundreds of vampires and we aren't all accountants, lawyers, or politicians. For example, I'm an academic and, as this account begins, a senior in the English Department at Harvard University circa 1972. My name is Iris, and I'm immortal.

Within the stately confines of Massachusetts Hall at just after 2:00 pm, Professor Allen was saying something about English governesses that I'd known since I was 600 years old. Thus I could moon over the true object of my attention without fear of missing something important. His name was David, and, as humiliating as it was for a centuries old creature of the night to admit, I was smitten. Worse still, I was too cowardly to do much more than smile dazedly into his brilliant blue eyes.

We'd spoken a few times before class, but those conversations —if one could call them conversations—rarely strayed far from pleasant greetings and *very* small talk. Once he'd asked me what I'd thought of the previous night's reading and I'd nearly died. Well, not *really*—I'd been there and done that, but it's a figure of speech. Now, I'd read that section of *Turn of the Screw* about 400 times, but when he'd flashed those baby blues on me every coherent thought in my ancient and staggeringly intelligent mind flew from me like so many bats.

But this day was different.

David was sitting in the second row nearest the window. His chestnut-colored hair sparkled in the sun, each glimmer of golden light flashing to reveal his auburn highlights and the few strands of premature silver. His lips were curled and his brow slightly furrowed as he shifted his focus in turns from his notes to Professor Allen and back again.

He was beautiful, with a dimpled chin, strong, Jeffersonian nose, and a long, well-formed neck that begged to be bitten—with passion rather than hunger, of course. A pair of horn-rimmed bifocals pinched his magnificent nose as he twirled his pen deftly between his long fingers. His skin was pale, not in an undead way, but with the alluring pallor that only hours in well-stocked, poorly lit libraries could provide. He was deep as an ocean, bright as a flash of lightning across a starless sky, and humble despite his obvious edge on the rest of his kind.

But I was not the only one who saw David for the miracle he was. Many of Harvard's young coeds nursed a soft spot for the brilliant and tantalizingly shy David ... and my least favorite of them was currently spoiling my view. Amanda Van Smute dropped her pencil on purpose and giggled coquettishly as David bent to pick it up for her.

"Whore," I hissed in a low whisper. Tim Spencer cast me a scandalized look from the desk on my left, but I paid him no mind. I was ancient and all-powerful; a snooty Cape Coder's views on my manners were far from the top of my list of cares. Thankfully, David reacted to little slutty Van Daddy's Money's fluttering fake eyelashes with indifference reminiscent of my own toward 'Trust Fund Timmy'.

I turned my attention momentarily back to Professor Allen. He was discussing allegory in late 19th century horror. His opinions were interesting enough for me to momentarily divert my focus from David and my now fervent desire to drain Amanda Van Smute until she was so dry I could use her corpse for kindling.

The campus bell tower clanged the end of the lesson just as Professor Allen was beginning to discuss *Dracula*. Banishing the rage that surged through me whenever Stoker's little 'hit piece' was mentioned, I gathered my notebook and my bag, and stood, making sure to linger as David copied down a final thought into his notes. Pretending to be engrossed in my own notes, I walked toward the door just as David made his way out of the classroom. With a thrilling surge of contact, we crashed together. Phase one of my master plan was complete.

"Oh, I'm so sorry," said David as he bent in a thrice to gather up my fallen papers and notebooks. "I wasn't looking where I was going, it was completely my fault."

I smiled into his blue eyes. It certainly wasn't his fault, but I wasn't going to be the one to say so. "Don't worry about it. You're David, right?" As if I didn't know …

He smiled; dear god was he dreamy! "Yeah," he answered, standing up and holding out a hand to help me do the same. "And you're Iris. I really like your input in class. You talk as if you're straight out of Victorian England."

If David only knew how right he was … I laughed and brushed his arm with my hand. "You caught me," I said. "I'm twenty-two going on two-hundred."

He joined me in laughter as we walked out into the hall together. I noticed Amanda glaring at me from the doorway as she turned to stalk toward the quad. I held back a smirk with great difficulty.

"I'm not sure we've officially met," said David shifting his books under his arm so that he could hold out a hand for me to shake. "I'm David Caldwell."

"Iris Ingoldsby," I answered as I gripped his hand in mine.

We were close enough for my highly developed senses to pick up his heartbeat. I was pleased to hear that it had quickened as our hands met; not so much that I feared dashing David would run off and engage my prey instinct—which was not ideal while trying to prove to a guy that you weren't only out for a quickie gulp of AB negative in the nearest supply closet—but enough that I knew he was thinking about more than Henry James.

David eyed me with some concern as we both let our hands fall back to our sides. "I don't need my jacket. You can borrow it if you're cold."

"Oh, don't worry about little old me," I said waving my icy hands before him. "I run cold." I'd discovered that was one of the nasty side effects of death. "I can warm up pretty quickly though. Where you off to next?"

"East side of campus."

"Me too," I lied. "Fancy a walking buddy? Things can be a bit dangerous for men on their own east of the Yard."

He laughed. "I'd like the company. Ingoldsby?" he said with the furrowed-browed smirk that meant he was doing some thinking. "Like the *Ingoldsby Legends?*"

"Nice reference, David Caldwell," I said, not even having to pretend to be impressed. So the boy knew his Victorian gothic literature? Be still my beat-less heart.

I'd lived many lives over the centuries, and had many names. I liked Iris Ingoldsby—I've always been a sucker for alliteration—but I was a senior now, and running out of time. Soon I would need to move on, and women who looked perpetually twenty-two could not risk long post-collegiate careers—not and avoid awkward questions.

"That's not a common name," added David as we trotted down the stairs to the ground floor side by side.

"I'm not a common girl."

"I can see that." David blushed scarlet.

I smiled. If he thought that little jape was too forward, he was in for quite the shock on our third date.

"Hold on," I said as David held the door out onto campus open for me. The sunlight was beating down on the grassy hills and glittering cobblestones as I fumbled for my glasses case. That whole 'vampire's getting burnt to a crisp by the sun' thing was pure poppycock, but that didn't mean an undead girl couldn't have sensitive eyes. They tended to get a bit ... well, *bloody* in direct sunlight. Resting my red-tinted Audrey Hepburn sunglasses in their proper, protective place, I stepped out into the world with David Caldwell.

We chatted happily as we passed by building after building and girl after jealous girl. I was surprised just how easy it was, now that I'd gotten over my initial jitters, to talk to him. We discussed books, music, and movies—the latter of which I was well-versed. given how easy it was to drain a bad date in the back of a dark theatre. Music, however ... Though I hadn't truly enjoyed a popular artist since Dvorak, I agreed that I'd listen to whoever Paul Simon was ... as long as David brought the record over to my place.

I'd laughed, I'd smiled, and I'd fluttered my eyelashes enough to cause a small hurricane, but as we approached Sever Hall— where David had his Renaissance Art elective—the familiar, pre-relationship worries began to build. Sure, we'd said we'd listen to a record together, but we hadn't settled on a time or day. Was he just being polite? What if he didn't want to take me out? What if I wasn't his type? What if he hated my hair this way and was desperate to fly from the girl with the freakishly long ponytail and toward those girls with the shorter hair he loved so much? What if I'd totally misread him and he was gay—not that there was anything wrong with that, but a girl likes to know a guy isn't thinking about Paul Newman while he's necking with her.

"I've got a question, Iris," said David quietly. "And I hope you won't think I'm too forward."

Dear God, I wouldn't have thought him forward if he wanted to take my bra off and hoist it up the nearest flag poll. "I'd rather you be forward than backward." I cringed slightly as I said that, but David laughed. Apparently my attempt to be 'cool and hip' hadn't failed too miserably. "Shoot, David."

"Do you want to have dinner with me ton—?"

"Yes!" I answered before he'd finished asking. I hoped, between my quickly affected cough and the passing raven I'd compelled into letting out a loud and perfectly timed caw, I could mask my enthusiasm.

"Sorry." David looked slightly terrified. "I didn't catch that. A bad time for a fly-by interruption."

Though I reveled in barely clinging to the high ground of cool, I resolved to a get a grip and fast. I wasn't some naive girl of 300 anymore. "No problem. Yeah," I said, trying to sound as if I wasn't tempted to dance a celebratory jig. "I'd like that."

The bell for the next lesson rang, but David paid it no mind. "What do you usually eat around here?"

"Um ..." I paused. The honest answer was not pretty. I'd taken to feeding primarily on frat boys. Nobody was the wiser if I drained a pint out of a guy who was already passed out ass-up on the sidewalks of fraternity row. They'd wake up with something not altogether worse than their usual hangovers and I'd manage a bit of a buzz from the booze in their blood. "I've been eating a lot of junk lately," I said with a sly smile. "I'm trying to be good, but ..."

David smiled in a knowing way. "You don't have to tell me how tempting fast food can be for the busy college student."

I laughed. Of course, those frat boys weren't moving all that fast after I was through with them, but ... "Yeah, fast food ... it can be murder."

David winked. "I know just the spot for a more substantial meal. There's a new Italian place in the Square. *Angelo's*. It's supposed to be the real deal, an authentic Tuscan place."

"I know it," I said. I didn't normally eat solid food, but Italian was my favorite to nibble on, and if the place was authentic, I could avoid the whole garlic issue. Real Italian cooks, like vampires, tended to avoid the stuff. "How about eight?"

David flashed a smile that brought an intoxicating twinkle to his blue eyes and an alluring tightening to the veins on his neck. Even if the only red I'd be sipping tonight would be from a bottle of Chianti Classico, a girl could still admire the goods. "I'll see you then, Iris," he said. "I'm Looking forward to it."

"Me too, David."

·　　　·　　　·

I could tell you about that date, about how handsome David looked, about how he really could fill out a pair of slacks, and dissected the wine list with the skill of an Italian count; and I could regale you with some highlights of our sparkling conversions, but I won't. I have some nice first date strategies that I'd begun perfecting long before Casanova had his first schoolboy crush. None of them are ... vampiric or anything, but a girl's tricks are her own, and nobody, whether eighteen or 800 liked to have their best stuff out in the open. Let's just say that our first date was a magical little evening that led to a second ... and a third.

I'd been tempted to break my three-date rule as we snuggled up together at the drive in, paying much more attention to each other than we were to the plot of *Diamonds are Forever*—which was probably for the best. Though I loved the feel of David's lips on mine, and hungered for more, both literarily and metaphorically, I resisted my two strongest urges and kept to my code. Nearly a millennium of experience had taught me a lot about relationships, and if Thomas Jefferson and Fredrick Douglass had had to wait three dates ... so would David Caldwell. My own moral proclivities aside, there was a far more vital reason that I always made sure to plan out my first time with a new guy.

In case you haven't been following along, I'm undead and thus don't have some of the natural qualities a man is accustomed to in a sexual partner. A satisfactory third date for an undead girl and her living partner comes with a hefty to-do list and more than a few costs for the surrounding human population. I had to 'fake it', you see. Not in the way that most girls 'fake it'—all those relevant areas were actually a bit keener now that I was no longer among the living; but there were certain areas were I was lacking ...

I had no heartbeat, I couldn't sweat, and achieving a normal human body temperature was simply a bridge too far on an average Friday. Each was a significant hurdle for me, a hurdle that required a bit of outside assistance to clear. So what if the Harvard basketball team felt a bit ... *drained* during the Ivy League tournament? David thought I was a real girl. That first night of tender, vulnerable normalcy was worth a thousand basketball teams ... to me at least. And, as an added bonus, my fangs were less likely to expand at an inopportune moment if I was properly satiated.

Six weeks after our first meal together in *Angelo's Authentic Tuscan Restaurant*, I found myself in a rare position, one I had never really held before. I'd bedded dozens of men over my immortal life, but I never realized just how hollow all of those moments had been until David Caldwell held me in his arms. I was nearing 800 years old, and, for the first time, I felt truly connected to someone else. I felt empty when we were apart—and that wasn't just because I was cutting down on the frat boys—and I found myself thinking about more than just the next escape to the next name and the next school. My time at Harvard was at an end. I knew that. I had to find the strength to cut the ties that bound me to this place, this time, and this life ... but that was proving difficult.

"Iris," said David, his reading glasses perched on his nose, a steaming mug of coffee in one hand, and a typed page of prose in the other, "this story is fantastic."

I eyed him suspiciously before dropping to my knees beside his seat on the couch and resting my head upon his bare shoulder. I nibbled his neck lightly, tasting a bit of the blood that had dried over the small wound I had left last night. He hadn't seemed to mind that I'd lost control and given him a bit more than a love bite in the final throws of our most recent passions. If anything, he seemed to have enjoyed the experience. "You don't need to flatter me, David. I'm already naked."

He turned and let his beautiful eyes scan my body. He grinned before kissing me. "So you are, but I won't be distracted. Not now. You have real talent, and for the life of me I don't know why you don't submit your work to magazines. I mean," he gave me a bemused look as he picked up page after page out of my cardboard box of finished stories, "every single one is a winner. Though some of the language in a few of these handwritten ones is a tad dated." He picked up a bundle of aged paper and held it out to me. "This one's like if Charlotte Bronte wrote for *Playboy*."

"Yeah," I said, my eyes flashing across the looping cursive that covered both sides of paper. "I was having a little fun with that."

"I like it." David laughed and placed the story I'd penned in 1849 back into the box. I hoped to God he hadn't read that one too careful. I'd published it under the name Sir Aloysius Benton-Knob more than a century ago. It had caught on in certain unsavory circles, been hailed as the first truly tasteful smut written since the glory days of Rome, and given rise to an enduring bit of phallic slang slightly less emasculating than 'willy.' "But seriously, Iris." David took my hand; even after all we've been to each other, I felt my icy skin warm at his touch. "These more recent stories ... You need to send them out. I mean, if I could write like you ..." he shook his head and let out a low whistle.

I sighed exasperatedly. "David, if you insist on talking business, instead of getting *down to it* on this couch, I'll have to put something on." I kissed David on the top of the head before grabbing my robe from the bedroom.

I stood in the doorway watching David Caldwell reading my writing. He had a look of mingled jealousy and pride splashed across his handsome face. There were plenty of good reasons I didn't usually publish my work. Sure there were a few of my stories, novels, essays, and criticism floating through the national consciousness, but none of them had ever been published using any name that could have been associated with me or any of my aliases. I'd not even allowed myself to write in a similar style through the years.

"I guess I could pretend to be a man," I said as I flopped down onto the couch beside him. Literary gender bending had always kept attention off me in the past.

David moved his glasses farther down his nose and stared over them shrewdly. "Why on earth would you do that?"

I hesitated for a fraction of a second, but thankfully humanity's age-old problem came riding chauvinistically to my rescue. "Nobody wants to read anything written by a woman."

"Tell that to Ayn Rand."

"You tell it to her," I answered sourly. Did he want me hunted down and staked? Or worse summoned by the Grand Vampiric Council and sentenced to two centuries in the 'Pit' for blowing my entire races cover ... *again?* I'd have much rather died than be subjected to the will of the Council a second time ...

"Or Dorothy Parker, or Agatha Christie, or Sylvia Plath—"

"If you want *me* to stick my head in an oven, you're going about it the right way!" I yelled.

I felt my fangs expand and quickly raised my hands up to cover my mouth. I didn't know why I was getting so angry. David couldn't know what he was asking me to do; and I'd published before, but I'd always had multiple layers of cover to protect my identity and my species. Anger was quickly replaced by terror as I saw David's eyes widen. He was looking at my mouth with an unreadable expression. I rolled my tongue superciliously over my canines to ensure they'd receded to a more human size before I lowered my hands and held one out to David. He took it in both of his own. His eyes flashed once toward my mouth again before he brushed his lips lightly against my slightly trembling hand. I stared at David with undisguised wonder. He must not have seen, he couldn't have or there was no way that he could—

Suddenly David's lips were on mine, and his arms were wrapping me in a tight embrace. I moaned as he pulled me closer, as his tongue met mine before lightly sliding across my ... I leapt back, startled.

"What?" he said breathlessly.

"Nothing." I knew I was blushing, and that in it itself was an achievement. I closed my mouth tight, afraid of what my biological imperative was producing in me. I knew my fangs had expanded as soon as David's tongue had touched them. I felt a powerful and very complicated urge to push David down and ravage him in more ways than one. I took a few deep, settling breaths before rising, shivering to my feet. "I'm sorry. I—"

"Why should you be sorry?" said David. He cupped my face in his hands and ran his thumb across my lips and over my now retracted fangs. "Why should you ever be sorry to show the world what you are?" He made to kiss me, but I backed away from his lips and his touch.

What I was? "Can't a girl be shy?" I asked. My heart, if it could beat, would have been pounding, but instead, I just felt a rush of blood building at my temples, threatening to spill over and make my eyes look like Christopher Lee's after a stake to the heart. "I just don't want the attention, okay?"

"Why not?" David was looking at me in a way that made even a vampire shiver.

"It's ... well ... I—"

David kissed me again. It was heaven to have his lips on mine, and it felt so damned good to be held, to be gripped in a warm embrace that sang of tenderness and even ... love.

"I always knew you were special," he said. "I knew it that first day in class. But when I saw the portrait—"

"What portrait?" My head was pounding and my vision had taken on a red tinge that not even my sunglasses could have matched. He couldn't mean the painting at—

"There's a painting at Brown ..."

I froze. There *was* a painting of me at Brown. Well, a painting of *late 15th century me* receiving a glass-ceiling breaking medical degree in Italy. It was the reason I'd never risked enrolling there. "Yes?"

"Well, I only know about it because my cousin." David furrowed his brow. "He's a doctoral candidate there. He seems to think that studying in front of this one woman's portrait gives him luck. He's a little bit in love with her, I think. He took me there, and when I saw it ..." David smiled. "Well, I couldn't blame him for falling for her. I certainly have. I thought at first that it just looked like you, maybe it was some distant relative, but the more time we spent together, Iris, the more I saw of *you* in that painting. And these stories ..." he gestured toward my trunk of fiction. "I know some of them, and I know you wouldn't copy down some obscure short stories just for the fun of it. These were published from 1827 to 1932 under different names and with different styles, but when I really started thinking about it, and looking at some of them again, I found a unique sound in the words." He grinned. "Your sound."

He knows ... "What are you trying to say, David?"

"That you've been alive for at least five hundred years, you're the best writer I've ever met, and that I love you."

I stared at him. The obvious questions and concerns regarding my own survival and perhaps a few decades in the Pit for punishment—maybe even a stake to the heart if the council was feeling vengeful—escaped me. I found myself brooding upon one word ... *love*. Lust, I could understand, but love? I'd never loved anyone during my undeath, and, as far as I knew, no one had loved me. My maker, Casto, had desired me, and imprisoned me for years, but he'd never loved anyone; Jefferson, for all his tender words, was ever Sally Hemmings' creature; and Frederick Douglas ... well, let's just say he had his hands full where women were concerned. In all my years, love had eluded me, was foreign to me. Perhaps it was beyond me. Love, which lived honestly in the bright glow of tender flame, could not belong to a child of the night, a lady of silence and shadow; but David knew what I was. He knew and had not run from me ... yet.

"David ..." My voice, to my surprise, was tremulous. "You don't know what I've done ... the lives I've lived, the lives I've ended."

"You're not a killer."

My fingers were around David's throat in a thrice. "All I have to do is squeeze to prove you wrong."

"You won't," David wheezed.

His eyes were on mine and I could feel that he believed that, that he trusted me ... that he loved me. He was pure. He was good. He deserved better than a woman who had to drain a dozen men to be warm for him. He deserved better than a girl whose heart would never quicken ... would never even beat for him. I'd been a fool to want him, a damned, selfish fool.

I threw him to the ground with a snarl. "Go!" I shouted. He didn't move. I rushed forward in a blur of rage and wind until I loomed over him, my fangs bared and ready for flesh. "Go!" I repeated savagely.

"You can't frighten me away." Tears were glistening in David's bright eyes. "Vampire or not, I love you, Iris!"

"That's not my name!" I spat.

"What is your name?"

Eiddwen ... Once my name was Eiddwen. It had been so long since I'd even thought of that name, of that life in Wales, of that poor, broken, terrified girl that had been shattered in shadow and remade in death. That girl had been taken from her parents, and from a man who had asked for her hand. God, I couldn't remember his face ... or even his name, but my father had approved the match ...

"I fell for Iris Ingoldsby," said David, not troubled by the fact that I hadn't answered his question, "but I'll love you no matter what you're called, no matter who you were, or what you are. I know you feel the same way."

Did I? Did I love—no—*could* I love David? "I'm a monster, David, you can't begin to comprehend what I feel, or what I'm capable of!"

"But I could! I'd have an eternity to learn everything about you and your—"

"Species!" I finished for him with a snap of my fangs. "You don't know what you're saying!" I sank onto the couch, my head in my hands. I had seen the deaths of everyone I'd ever cared for, and after years of toil had learned that it was best not to care. It was best to seal my heart away rather than see it shattered. I'd seen war, and plague, and chaos … I'd lived a thousand hells on earth and done my own devilry just to avoid the black nothing that surely awaited me in true death.

"You'd be giving up your very soul, David. You couldn't live, not truly. You'd be running all your days, changing names and stories just when you've figured out how to exist in your current manufactured life. You'd be alone forever."

"No." David smiled and held my hand in his. "Neither of us would be alone … ever again."

How tempting it was to fall into the dream that David spun, that heaven for the damned, that rare glimmer of hope for the hopeless. He and I could be together. I could finally have a cold companion to warm my undeath until the end of all things; but at what cost to a man who loved me? Perhaps his heart would harden in death, and when he was born anew in frigid darkness he wouldn't know himself. My humanity had been taken from me, and for all my time, my knowledge, my adventures, I wished for nothing more than to have that spark of mortality … of humanity back again.

"I didn't choose this life," I said quietly.

"But I'll choose it." David smiled. "I'll chose it if it means I can be with you."

"I wouldn't wish this on my worst enemy. God, David! You won't be human, you'll have nothing, no one—"

"But you."

"Would that be enough?" I asked, my eyes on his, my stomach fluttering nervously. What did I want? "We can't have children. We won't have friends for longer than a few years. We can't have a home." I hadn't known a home since Wales, but with David … with David perhaps I could find home, not in a place, but in a person. I gave my head a firm shake … I couldn't afford to be weak. Not now. "What about your parents, your family?"

"I never met them," he said coldly. "I was in an orphanage until I was six and then I was adopted by an old couple in Michigan. The Caldwells."

"Are the Caldwells still in Michigan?" He had people who cared for him, people who would search for him and ask questions if he were to disappear. When David nodded, I was relieved and devastated in equal and confusing measure, still unsure of just what I wanted ... of just what he was to me; but then he spoke:

"They're six feet under," he said. "In adjoining plots in St. Luke's Cemetery in Lansing. I gave the eulogy during my junior year of high school. They were good people." His blue eyes weren't wet. That wound had closed. At least I hoped that was the case. It was better than not grieving, than not feeling.

I remembered going back to my old home in Wales, after I'd decapitated my master and thrown his head into a river for good measure. The small garden, always full of chickens, and the two craggy fields flecked with my father's sheep were empty and overrun by weeds. A sign had hung over the door that day, with two words written in red: DAMNED. SUICIDE. My parents were still there when I opened the door. They were bones after all that time, their skeletal hands joined and a knife at my father's side.

The damned parents of a damned daughter, driven to take their own lives by the disappearance of their only child—and twice damned that that daughter still lived. I hadn't cried. I didn't mourn. There wasn't enough human left in me to grieve for those rare few who had loved me; but now another held me in his heart and I felt, if not love, than an attachment for him—a desperate connection of a cold heart to one still warmed by love.

"I'm sorry about the Caldwells," I said, trying to remember what true remorse, true compassion, felt like. "Brothers? Sisters?"

"No." David smiled rather sadly. "I'm all alone. Just like I was at the beginning, but I don't want to be alone anymore."

David Caldwell was an orphan. He was lost. He was the perfect prey—at least that's what I would have thought if he were anyone else. David knew what he wanted, but did I?

He deserves better than this life, cried a voice of reason in my mind, *He isn't broken, not yet.* Perhaps it was voice of that girl in Wales who had never wanted this, who had died afraid and been born anew in rage and sorrow.

But what if David Caldwell wanted to be broken? Broken and remade? What if he was just as afraid right now as I'd been in a dark cell nearly eight hundred years ago? I'd prayed for a hero, a knight, or an angel to bring me into the light of day, to end my pain in the darkness, but no one had come and I had been forced to seek comfort in the shadows I'd once feared. Perhaps David's fear of desertion, of solitude, was such that he would take endless days of secrecy in the shadows over finite uncertainty in the sun.

"You'd really choose to be like me?"

David's hands were suddenly in mine. "If it means I can be *with* you, yes."

I smiled, hoping that the damned could be saved, and that the dead could still love. I knew it was wrong to take the spark of life from him just to bring some hollow warmth to my empty heart, and thoughtless to take him at his word, but David Caldwell was tired of being alone ... and so was I.

I won't tell of the turning. It's far too intimate and rather disgusting if you aren't one of my kind. David awoke from death and was the same man, with the same heart and the same misguided affection for a girl who had lived far too many lifetimes; but David and Iris weren't long for this world. Five years after David's turning, we both 'died' in a car crash before laying low for a few decades in a nice secluded cabin in the mountains of Bolivia.

Now it's 1999, David and I are together in Dublin—both history students at Trinity College. After centuries on the hunt, skulking from shadow to shadow and running from my past, I remember, at long last, what it's like to be home. I've been Eiddwen, Sarah, Francesca, and countless others. I've lived in pain and sorrow, cursing my unending years until they brought me David. For him, I'll be Iris forever; I will live, and at long last love.

THE DATE

Valerie Cullers

ANNALEA FLOPPED into the nearest chair in the living room. She had been cleaning the kitchen and it was *finally* finished. It had taken her a couple of days to wash the walls and clean out the refrigerator and the oven. Her work was finished for the day and after a short rest, she wanted to go up to the park and walk.

Thirty minutes later, she slipped on her tennis shoes, opened the back door, and headed up the hill to the park. It had a great walking path and she enjoyed letting the stress of the day go as she completed each lap. She got on the path and noticed that Ron, a man she walked with a few days ago, was also on the path. She waved and he waved back. A few minutes later, he caught up to her and they walked together for the next half an hour.

They shared pleasantries but nothing very personal except their first names. He looked like he was a little older than her oldest son. "So, Ron, where do you work?" she asked.

"I'm on winter leave from The Fish and Wildlife Service," he answered. "Most of the birds have flown south for the winter and there is not much to do until spring."

She looked at him closely. He was wearing a red and black flannel shirt and blue jeans. She had thought he probably worked at one of the three lumber mills in town. "That's a great job for someone who loves the outdoors," she remarked.

"Yes, it is. And you, what do you do for a living?" he asked.

"I am retired. I'm just back in town to clean up my parents' house and put it on the market. I haven't lived here since I was a teenager," she answered.

"That must be a chore," he remarked.

"Yes, it is. It's been a rental for the past few years since they passed. The renters took good care of it but everything still needs a good scrubbing," she replied.

They continued walking and chatting and Ron asked her where she lived. She told him and headed down the hill to fix her dinner and watch TV for the rest of the evening. Several minutes later, she heard a knock on the front door. She looked out and there stood Ron. She opened the door slowly, "Ron, what are you doing here?"

"I don't know. I guess I thought you could use a good dinner this evening," he said.

She looked at him for a moment. "I don't know. I'm leaving tomorrow to go home for the weekend. My daughter is having a birthday party and I want to be there to help her celebrate."

"Come on. I'll pick you up at 5:00 and take you out for a good steak. You like steak, don't you?" he asked.

"Yeah, I do." She looked down the street and saw his four-wheel drive pickup. It was clean and looked in good condition. "I don't even know your last name."

"It's Reddington. You can Google me and make sure I'm on the up and up," he said with a laugh.

Annalea stood there for a moment. She had felt safe with Ron when she walked with him the last few days. When a jogger or biker passed them, he always moved her out of the way to protect her. She checked her gut and she had a good feeling about him. If nothing else, she had learned to trust her gut feelings about people. "Okay, I'll see you about 5:00."

Ron laughed. "Great, see you then." He turned and walked down the steps that led up to the house.

As soon as he was out of sight, Annalea Googled him. There was nothing negative about him online and he had won an award for helping an endangered species in the area. It reassured her that he was probably okay. In her suitcase was a nice pair of grey pants and a light pink top. She dressed, washed her face, put on lipstick, and combed her hair. "Maybe I'll get a new friend out of this deal," she thought to herself.

Ron knocked on the door exactly at 5:00. "Good for him," Annalea thought. "I hate it when people are late." He wore a nice pair of jeans, dress shirt, and a jacket. He looked good and she would have been proud to call him a friend. He took her to Barnaby's, the local steak pit in town.

Throughout the meal, they shared more about themselves and Annalea felt comfortable opening up a little bit more with him.

"Would you like dessert?" he asked.

"No, but I could use a cup of coffee," she answered.

He ordered one for both of them and then looked at her for a while. Finally, he said, "Annalea, when you get back in town, I would like to take you out again."

Annalea laughed. "Uh, Ron, how old are you?"

"Fifty-one," he said.

"And how old do you think I am?" she asked.

"M-m-m, a few years older than me. Fifty-five or so," he replied.

Annalea laughed again. "Ron, I am sixty-five. Fourteen years older than you."

"You're kidding!" Ron said and his face turned red. "I can't believe it."

Annalea pulled out her Driver's License and showed him. "Ron, this is truly such a sweet gesture. I am flattered that you would think of me in this way. I thought you just wanted to be friends."

Ron remained quiet as she finished her coffee. "I'm ready to go if you are," she said. Ron paid the bill and they left the restaurant. He drove her home and walked her to the front door. "Ron, thanks so much for dinner. I won't forget it."

Ron left and Annalea went into the house. She finished packing for her trip home the following day. She enjoyed the weekend with her daughter and shared the story about Ron with her. They both got a good laugh out of it. At the end of the weekend, she returned to her parents' house. The next day she got up and began tackling the living room. There wasn't much to do in this room, just vacuuming and wiping down the walls. About noon, she heard a knock on the door. She looked outside and it was Ron. She opened the front door and went out onto the porch.

"Hi Ron, what's up?"

"I've thought about it a lot this past weekend and I'm in if you are," he said.

Annalea looked at him. He certainly looked serious. "Ron, this couldn't work for so many reasons, but primarily it is our age gap. Why I could have a stroke or a heart attack and be gone tomorrow."

"I know. I've thought about it, and I'm in. I've never met anyone like you and I am willing to see where this could take us," he said.

Annalea looked at him and shook her head. "Ron, you don't know what you are saying. In ten years, you will be sixty-one and I will be seventy-five."

"I know. It doesn't matter to me. I want to try and make this work," he reiterated.

"I have never even dated since my husband and I got divorced," she said. "Men have been on my taboo list."

"Just think about it," he said. He handed her a slip of paper with his name and phone number on it. "Call me." He turned and walked down the steps and got into his truck.

She watched until his truck was out of view. She shook her head and walked back into the house. Should she even entertain the idea? She looked at the slip of paper he gave her. There was a list of possibilities associated with it, some wonderful and some terrifying. Should she risk it? Her heart took her one way then her head reeled her back the other. She would have to think long and hard before she made a decision.

Annalea picked up the handle of the vacuum and continued vacuuming. When she finished, she sat back down in the chair. Elation, dread, excitement, worry ... each emotion flooded over her. Did she have the courage to risk it, to risk getting hurt again with someone who might reject her as she aged?

Annalea didn't know but she would certainly enjoy entertaining the idea of finding love again. Instead of her walk today, Annalea decided she would go down to Blake's Hardware. She had a friend from high school who worked there. This was a small town and she knew that Becka would have the scoop on anyone who lived there.

She stood at the counter and could see through the office window that Becka was there today. Becka looked up and waved. She came out in a hurry. "Annalea, what are you doing here?"

"I'm cleaning up my folks' house because I am going to put it on the market."

"Can I help you find anything?" Becka asked.

Annalea leaned into the counter and whispered, "I really would just like to talk with you."

Becka looked around. "Let's go next door for a cup of coffee."

Annalea followed Becka next door to the diner. They sat down and soon a waitress came and took their order. "So, what's up? I haven't seen you in a few years," Becka said.

"I want some information on someone," Annalea began.

"Oh, tell me more," Becka said and laughed.

"What do you know about Ron Reddington?"

"Oh, the town's most eligible bachelor? Quite a bit really. He started remodeling his house a few years ago and he comes into the store a couple of times a week. For starters, he's the rugged outdoor type, most everyone likes him and he's dated several women. But none of his relationships seem to go past the third or fourth date. He loses interest quickly in most women. How did you meet him?" Becka asked.

"I've been walking on the trail in the park above my parents' house and he and I have walked together for several days. He asked me to dinner last week and I thought it was just to be friendly. Towards the end of dinner, he said he wanted to start dating me."

"Does he know how old you are?" Becka asked.

"Now he does. He thought I was about five years older than him. I told him I was flattered but our age difference was too much. He showed up today on my front porch and said he doesn't care and that he still wants to give us a shot."

Becka sat back in the booth. "I'm flabbergasted. Most women pursue him and he doesn't show a lot of interest. Now, he's the one pursuing you? That gives you an edge in my book."

"I don't even know what to think. After Stan left me for his secretary, I had sworn off men altogether. The thought of having another relationship with someone and possibly finding love went totally out the window. I know it seems crazy but when I think of him, I suddenly feel alive."

"Well, who wouldn't? Becka said.

"Fourteen years, Becka, fourteen years, that's the difference between us. Just think."

"Yes, it could all go terribly wrong or it could be the most special relationship you ever had," Becka added.

"Well, the one good thing people in my family have going for them is that most of them don't live past eighty."

"It would be a leap of faith, Annalea, but what a leap," she said.

Annalea thought for a few moments. "Yes, you're right. I'll have to give it a lot of thought. Now, tell me about your family."

Becka started in with the details and finished up with, "But nothing is as exciting as what we have been talking about."

Annalea laughed. "You always did know how to cut to the chase. I knew I could count on you to give me the pertinent details about him. Hey, mum's the word on this. I haven't decided what I am going to do."

"Of course. Thank God I don't believe in gossip or I would have lots to get the hens cackling this afternoon. Speaking of cackling, I had better get back to the shop or they'll wonder what happened to me."

"Thanks, Becka. I knew I could count on you."

Annalea picked up a few items at the hardware store and then went back to the house. She thought about Ron the rest of the afternoon and made a decision. She picked up her phone and dialed his number. "Hi."

"Hi," he answered

"Well, I've been thinking about us a lot and I thought if you want, we could just be friends. I have to be here for another few weeks and we could do some fun things together during that time"

"It's something but not what I really want," he said.

"It's up to you. I like you but I don't see much of a future for us in a long-term relationship."

He was quiet for several seconds and then sighed. "I guess something is better than nothing. What do you say we go down to the refuge tomorrow and I'll show you around."

Annalea caught herself before she said, "Okay, it's a date." Instead, she said, "Sure, sounds fun. What time do you want to pick me up?"

"How about 11:00. We can drive around and then have lunch at the café there," he said.

They spent a lot of time together during the next two weeks. She would work on her parents' home in the morning and then see him either on the walking trail in the afternoon or they would set up something more specific. The last night they went to dinner at a nice Italian restaurant. When they finished, he drove her home and walked up the stairs to her porch. "You're awfully quiet," she remarked.

"I just don't think you are taking me seriously. You don't think I could take care of you when you are older," he said dejectedly.

She could see the hurt on his face. She brushed his cheek with her hand. "Ron, it's not that I don't think you could take care of me or that you would; it's that I wouldn't ask that of you."

He put his hands on her shoulders. "Could I please kiss you once before you leave?"

She thought for a few seconds. "Yes."

He leaned in and kissed her gently. She returned the kiss and his kiss became more intense and urgent. She could feel the electricity pass between them. She pulled away, "Wow!"

"That's what I have been trying to tell you. There is something special between us. I can feel it." He turned away and walked down the stairs. When he was at the bottom of the stairs, he said, "Think about it."

Annalea smiled. She was shaken at what had just taken place between them. She turned and went into her parents' house. She would think about it but she knew she would come up with the same answer.

She finished packing and drove home the next day. When she walked into her house, she saw she had several messages on her answering machine. After she put down her purse and suitcase, she sat at the counter and listened to them. The one that caught her attention was the one that said, "Annalea, this is Dr. Fargason. There was a spot on your mammogram, please call me and we will schedule a diagnostic mammogram and possibly a biopsy."

She fixed herself a cup of coffee and went into the living room to think about the message. She wanted to call Ron and tell him about it but dismissed the thought out of hand. Instead, she called her daughter and told her. The next two weeks were a blur as she had the biopsy, met with an oncologist, scheduled a PET Scan, met with the oncologist again and scheduled a mastectomy. The decisions weren't hard to make, it was just tiring going from one doctor or procedure to another.

She gave herself the next week off to think and prepare for the mastectomy. She had made some pretty life-altering decisions but really she felt, the decisions were practically made for her with the diagnosis from the oncologist. She thought about Ron a lot that week and made a decision. She picked up her phone and dialed his number, "Hi Ron,"

"Hi Annalea, I was hoping to hear from you."

"Well, I have some good news and some bad news."

"Please give me the bad news first," he said.

"I had a mammogram and they found a spot on it. It turned out to be a fairly aggressive form of cancer. I've scheduled a mastectomy for next week,"

"Annalea, I'm so sorry," he said. "Will you need radiation or chemotherapy?"

"The Doc said with this kind of cancer I have three to four years. Chemo or radiation will only add about six months to my life and I would be sick for the first year. It's just not worth it."

"What else did the doctor say?" he asked.

"He said I should be good for most of that time. The last few months will be a bit rough because this kind of cancer goes to your lungs and it makes it hard to breathe."

"My Gosh, how are you dealing with it?" he said.

"I don't feel too bad about it. I've lived my life, raised my kids and spent time with my grandkids. Any time left is a real bonus for me."

He was quiet for a few moments, then said, "Have you thought any more about us?"

"Well, that's the good news. Since I won't be around for another decade or so. I would be willing to get to know you better and see if there is some sort of future for us, however brief it may be. So, now I would say to you, think about it."

"I will Annalea, I promise," he said.

"I'm going to say goodbye. I'm pretty tired."

"Goodbye, Annalea, get some rest," he said.

Annalea put down her phone and went into the bedroom to lie down. She felt good inside. She wasn't sad about everything that was happening, just relieved that she had finally made a decision about Ron. No matter what his answer would be, she had given him a chance. She fell asleep within a few minutes and heard her phone go off in the kitchen. She didn't want to get up and see who it was. She let herself rest and got up about an hour and a half later.

When she finally wandered into the kitchen for another cup of coffee, she looked at her phone. She had missed a call from Ron and there was a message. She listened to the message. "Annalea, this is Ron. I'm in. I'm all in. I want to spend whatever time we can together from here on out and I want to be there for the surgery. Call me."

She smiled. She would call him back in a while but for now, she would bask in the glow of knowing she was loved and not alone as she faced her future. God was so good, so good indeed. She sat there thanking God for Ron and what he meant to her and what he might mean to her as the future unfolded. She picked up the phone, took a deep breath, and dialed his number.

OF LEATHER AND WOOL

Cameron E. Quinn

I T'S A COMMON MISCONCEPTION that selkies come in a single flavor—cute little harbor seals with their freckles and pudgy, pinchable cheeks—but they aren't the only pinnipeds who can shed their coats for a little land-lubbering.

I started porpoising to pick up speed, slicing in and out of the Salish Sea, kicking up a frothy wake as I plunged between the frigid saltwater and the sweltering radiance like some remix of a Roman bath. *I could really go for a human-style spa day.*

The journey had taken us weeks; I knew in every aching muscle why we selkies typically moved into San Francisco during mating season instead of joining this migration. The increasing smell of oil and partially-treated sewage, signs that Seattle was near, made me want to cry for so many reasons. If I added a little extra saline to the sea, who would know?

Around what I hoped was Port Madison (I couldn't exactly pull out a GPS in this form) I broke away and swam through the squirrely currents of Agate Pass. There was a selkie-friendly home on the west side of Bainbridge Island where I hoped to haul out and pick up the packages I'd mailed to myself. I recognized the stretch of beach I was looking for and flopped out of the water, shifting into shorts with a leather belt just to soak up the sun and rest for a minute.

My human physique has been described as a beardless dad-bod Momoa, which I took as high praise until recently. I'm solidly over six feet tall and muscular, but my abs are safely tucked away under a smooth layer of blubber. Only my cheekbones and angular nose are what one would call strongly defined. My tanbark complexion is nowhere near as dark as my chocolate brown fur, but it would get closer if I spent more of my human hours outside. Computers and daylight don't play well together.

My pickled skin started to feel stretched and itchy in the extended dose of sun; my human form was still vulnerable and reminded me to keep moving as much as my sea lion instincts had. I picked up my packages: my wallet, some socks (all novelty), my trusty pair of goes-with-everything leather boots, and a new phone. Mine had met an unfortunate, watery end around the time I decided to swim up the coast. No, I hadn't forgotten it in a pocket while shifting; not this time. It had been thrown. By me. For the crime of delivering a message I didn't want to hear then and didn't want to think about now.

I had memorized the only number I needed (and one more I'd never be calling again), and called it as promised.

"Hi Mom," I tried to sound chipper for the voicemail despite my exhaustion. "I arrived safe and sound in the Sound," heh, "and got my new phone—obviously. Love you."

My stupid human fingers almost dialed the other number. *Don't make me turn you back to flippers.* I shoved the phone into my pocket.

I took the ferry the rest of the way into Seattle. I could get one of those waterproof cases on a lanyard and hope some helpful boaters didn't try to rescue 'the poor sea lion' from entanglement, but it was harder to find a safe place to shift in a city. We selkie are supposed to be fictitious, after all. It was best not to let any of the full-time humans in on the secret.

Besides, I wanted to play at being human for a while.

I was so used to surrounding myself with other sea lions even when I was shoreside; I'd need to break that habit if I wanted to avoid my ex. Have I mentioned what a small world the selkie community is? That lack of personal boundaries you see on the buoys and docks doesn't go away when we shift. A lot of who we are stays the same.

For instance, I do modeling by trade in both my forms. My most dependable work is posing for tourists at Pier 39. My aunties have been modeling there since the Loma Prieta earthquake of '89. It's a paid-in-room-ON-boards gig. Ahem, you know, because of the wooden floating docks they ... never mind.

I ignored every muscle aching for a nap and continued walking inland, up to Capitol Hill. I was determined to dive right in, expecting this change of scenery would turn everything around for me. Ridiculous, unreasonable, pin-your-hopes-on-a-sea-star expectations. They were dashed.

Capitol Hill hit like the light beer version of San Francisco. I know they'd rather be known as the microbrew to our cosmo. If I were comparing all of Seattle? Sure. But Capitol Hill felt like it had the intent of the Castro with none of the flavor. Maybe I just didn't know where to look.

Maybe I'd just swum 930 nautical miles up the coast to find something *different.* Did I think of that? No. I moped in some cute purple building off Olive, watching groups of happy drunks sing karaoke to each other on the far side of the Seattle freeze. I finished my beer and left.

I hoped a good night's sleep would help set me on a less melancholic track in a different neighborhood of Seattle. The hotel was nice enough, certainly more comfortable on a human back than the piles of rocks I'd been sleeping on, but the sheets felt very cold.

·   ·   ·

We were at the peak of summer, but Seattle still managed to slip me a rainy, gray day. It suited me just fine. I glamoured myself into a coffee-brown leather jacket, rented a bike, and rode through the drizzle to Discovery Park. Damp and empty.

I didn't swim all this way to wallow. I meandered my way to Fisherman's Terminal, where I assumed I could find some good seafood. I picked a pub with a big patio full of cafe tables, all unoccupied, and popped in for a menu.

"Would you like to sit at the bar or a table?"

"No outdoor seating?"

The host chuckled and picked up a menu. "Good one. Does that mean you want a window seat, hon?"

I laughed along and nodded as if I hadn't meant to sit outside in the rain. My coat kept me plenty warm in Puget Sound, but I had to remind myself that humans were far more sensitive to the chill. I busied myself on my phone looking for contract gigs. *Please let there be plenty to keep me distracted.* If I could just drown myself in work, I wouldn't have time to feel lonely. The view out the window persisted in its gloom.

A bark of laughter drew my attention to a man chatting with the bartender while lackadaisically watching the baseball game. Apparently the Mariners were in Pittsburgh. I couldn't have cared less about what was happening on that field; I felt like I'd just struck upon a diamond.

I gulped the last few inches of my beer and moved to the bar to order another myself. The man who'd caught my ear was short and stocky, with cheeks that rose up round and red when he laughed. His face was covered with freckles, the fat kind that bled into each other like dappled shadows, and the tawny brown hair that escaped his wool cap was streaked with silver. Best of all, he smelled of the sea. Fish guts and over-ripe seaweed, salt and a hint of diesel.

He *had* to be a selkie. A harbor seal selkie. The cutest kind.

My little nerdy heart swooned.

Then I froze. This was uncharted territory. I couldn't remember the last time I'd flirted with someone I hadn't been introduced to by a mutual acquaintance. I looked up at the television, wondering if I could scrounge up some reasonable commentary. Nah, why bother starting somewhere that would never be common ground?

"Did you want another blonde?" The bartender asked.

No, I want to try the going-gray. Obviously the wrong answer, it still gave me an idea. "I wanted to try something different, something local," and then I boldly turned to the man in the wool cap. "You look like a man of excellent taste; what are you drinking?"

I was internally screaming so loud that I didn't even hear his response, but I nodded to the bartender and got a pale ale out of the deal. I took a sip and tried to build up the nerve to make the next move. Thank the sea stars I didn't have to.

"Where you from?" The man in the wool cap asked, amiable as a porpoise.

"San Francisco."

"You just visiting?"

"For now, but I'm assessing the feasibility of relocation and gathering data for a cost-benefits analysis." I slapped a palm over my eyes and groaned. "I'm sorry, I just jumped into work mode. Pretend I said that in human."

The man laughed. Hard.

I took that as a good sign. "I'm Kautak."

"Mortimer Crewe," he answered and held out his hand. "Or Tim, if you're anyone but my mother." We shook.

"So, what do you do, Tim?"

"Fish."

"Fishing, huh? Do you ever just go wild and grab a few with your teeth, or do you stick to the nets?"

Tim barked a laugh. "Neither, actually. I'm on an Alaskan longliner; *Josephine Kelpie*."

"You work in Alaska? And I thought *my* commute was bad. That's one helluva swim!"

He laughed again.

It was a good thing I was practicing on a selkie. This conversation would have been mortifying if I'd been talking to a human. I should probably be trying harder to sound like a full-timer, though, for the sake of practice. *What would a human say?*

"Do you have any favorite ... docks?"

"Docks? You mean, ports?"

You know, places to haul out, with all the other Seattle selkies? But the bartender was easily within range of our conversation so I couldn't say that. "Or, uh ... beaches?"

"For fishing off of, y'mean? I dunno, I do so much fishing on the boss's dime, it's the last thing I'd want to do on my own time. Sorry."

"Not necessarily to fish from. Just to, y'know, *enjoy the water?*" Did this guy really not know what I was getting at? Or was he just shy about letting on. Nowhere's got San Francisco beat for cryptid acceptance, but I didn't think the Seattle freeze was dangerous to our kind.

"Golden Garden's nice, or Gasworks if you want something with a view of the skyline." The conversation lulled for a moment, then Tim asked, "So what do you do?"

"Freelance modeling."

"The 3-D kind or the ... charts and stuff?"

I tried not to be offended that he didn't assume fashion modeling. I was in my human form, after all. "Charts and stuff. Recently created a set of population projections for the Sportfishing Association of California."

"Hah," he acknowledged without enthusiasm. *Come on, what kind of selkie didn't get excited about fish?* "Those coddled little trophy hunters."

Ahhh. Now I was getting the sway of the water.

"Would you believe that—when I went to deliver my findings—there was a man complaining that his wife wanted 'more of the pretty ones' on their next trip?"

He wheezed with laughter. "Was she talking about the garibaldi or the young 'instructors'?"

"My Mom says garibaldi are like those fancy wedding cakes—pretty on the outside, not worth eating on the inside."

"Now I don't know if I've ever met a cake not worth eating."

"Then, clearly, you haven't had a moon wrasse."

"Huh?"

"Oh, I thought we were talking about cakes metaphorically."

"Hah! Metaphorical cakes ..."

I found that I really enjoyed making Tim laugh. And it wasn't just because his freckles rode the crinkling of his face like sea birds bobbing on the swell. The sound of it was as predictable as thunder—at times a boom, or a long soft rumble, or a clap so very like a harbor seal I did a double take to make sure he was still in his human coat—but always following a flash of something I'd said. It made me feel brilliant, even though he was probably laughing at what an idiot I would have sounded like to a full-timer. Maybe someday I would push myself out of my comfort zone and have a conversation like this with someone who wasn't a fellow cryptid, but I was glad today didn't need to be that day.

"So, speaking of food ..." in for a herring, in for a tuna, right? "What restaurants do you recommend around here ... and can I buy you dinner at one of them?"

This earned me another of Tim's barks. "You California folk are a different breed."

I almost clarified that yes, technically I am a sea lion ... but the bartender was clearing our empty pint glasses. So instead I just laughed with him.

Collective shouts over an evasive pop fly effectively removed us from my inquiry. Maybe I'd misread him. Maybe Tim wasn't into men like that. Not that I would have minded just being friends (the wiser decision for my tender heart) but once you insert flirtation into a conversation, it's harder to remove than a limpet from its favorite rock.

"So, clearly you're not a vegetarian," Tim indicated my second order of fish. "I know a place that's pretty good, if you're looking for something distinctly Ballard."

We exchanged phones. I put a sea lion emoji after *Kautak*. When I hit save, my gaze lingered on the home screen and its portrait of a salmon-tailed merman with fiery red hair and a huge beard rivaled only by his smile. *Fishsticks*, was Tim already taken?

Tim caught me looking. "Ah! Yeah, my friend works in modeling too!" Tim laughed at his own joke; I tried not to be mad that I had to scratch it off my list.

It was awfully brazen to just have a picture of a merrow on his phone like that, where anyone could see it. The bartender, for instance. "I have the whole calendar. Those guys look like a lot of fun. I was thinking maybe Seattle needs a chapter." He stroked his beard.

As the bartender and Tim chatted about beard care, I was suddenly very aware of beards' aversion to growing on my face. Was Tim into facial hair? Was I not his type? The fried fish felt heavy in my gut.

•　　　•　　　•

The restaurant was on a cool, tree-lined street with surprisingly moderate traffic considering how delicious everything on the block looked. Most delicious of all was Tim. I had the distinct impression that he had dressed up, Seattle casual style. The shirt was free of wrinkles and the classic maritime stains of engine grease and fish guts. He still smelled of pine tar, but in a sweet-and-spicy way that made me wonder if it had come from a bar of soap. His beard was combed and shimmered a little. I imagined his hands running the beard oil through the salt-and-pepper tendrils. Then I imagined my hands ... *nope,* I reeled myself in.

The bar's sign had a cute hops bud wearing a horned hat—the kind Vikings never wore—but inside, a Viking figurehead mounted above the fireplace gave the impression that a whole ship might come crashing through the stone wall. *Hmmm, a beautiful old wooden boat full of burly old Vikings?* That sounded like a good time.

Tim caught me grinning. "It's great, huh? Wait until you see the menu. And taste their mead."

Normally I'm more surf than turf, but if orcas can eat us, I think I'm entitled to eat a pig every once in a while. I was glad I opted for something other than seafood once Tim started telling stories of his misadventures on the Bering Straits. It was enough to put even a selkie off his fish.

When he'd started counting off the sailors he'd known with missing digits, I interjected "two more and you'll run out of fingers!"

"One more if the unlucky sailor's me!"

We both barked with laughter.

Once we'd drained our rustic ceramic tankards for the third time, we declared ourselves stuffed to the gills and ready to wander the streets of Ballard. I wanted to hold his hand, or wrap an arm around his shoulder, but I played it cool.

"Awww, would y'look at that ..." I pointed to a lamp in a window that's base looked like a pair of harbor seals chasing each other around a clump of bull kelp. Then I crinkled my brow at the clown-shaped mug next to it. "What kind of store is this?"

"Let's check it out." Tim held the door open for me. Inside was a wild selection of furniture and decor from every style that has ever existed, and probably a few that were never fashionable anywhere.

I've often extolled the flexibility of having few physical belongings. Full-timers invested far too many resources in having stuff for the sake of it. Yet I had spent my life surrounded by other selkies' things. Suddenly, a little worm wriggled in my stomach whispering, *You've been letting other people call the shots.*

Would buying this funky coffee table made out of driftwood and broken CDs help me to be more assertive? Probably not. But just looking at it brought me a little surge of unexpected joy. I imagined a life in which I could set precisely what I wanted on that table. My heart bobbed out of sync with the steady roll of swells, like a tsunami warning buoy keying in on something that could be big ... or nothing.

Tim noticed my keen attention to the table. "Now that's something! I'd have a hard time fitting it in my berth, though."

He got us both laughing and moving along to the next novelty. Here we were, two men, decades into our adult years without ever having a place to call our own. Maybe those bird shifters were onto something. Nesting seemed kinda fun.

We treated the store like a playground. We held up silly hats, pretended to be Gen Zs trying to identify the function of a bubblegum pink rotary phone, puzzled over antiques we really didn't understand. I laughed so long I felt it in my abs.

"Oh. My. Cod." I pulled up short at a particular painting and grabbed Tim's shoulder so he could gawk with me. At first glance, it was the kind of old-timey portrait from the 1700s with too many people in too many ruffles that I never would have glanced twice at if my mother hadn't loved taking me to museums. Then I noticed the cryptid.

"Well that's ... interesting," Tim responded wryly.

"It's ... it's a computer programmer joke," I burbled. "It's Hogarth's *Tavern Scene*, but with a lion shifter in the place of Tom Rakewell. Oh my cod, *Tom Cat* ... it just keeps getting better ..."

Tim offered me a crooked smile, like he *wanted* to laugh but ...

"It's a CAD CAT!" I barked. "As in, computer-aided design, computer-aided ... testing ..."

Unbidden, a memory echoed in my head. *Yeah, we had some fun, but I'm looking for a beach master now, and you're still acting like an over-eager pup.* The grin slid from my face.

"Don't." Tim's voice was soft, but firm.

"I'm sorry," I mumbled, totally deflated.

"No, no, that's the opposite of what I meant. Don't be embarrassed that you got excited about something."

My eyes watered up, so I faked a sneeze to try and disguise it. I hadn't put anything as useful as a tissue into my glamoured up pocket, but then there Tim was, holding out a handkerchief like some knight in shining armor. I know he saw my tears, but he didn't get all awkward or macho about it.

"Woo, it sure is dusty in here," I lied anyway. For my sake. The night had been so perfect; I didn't want it to end with me a blubbery mess.

Tim yawned and made his it's-getting-late excuses. Maybe as much of a lie as my sneeze, but I couldn't blame him. Before the grit in my gut had time to turn itself into a stone, however, Tim asked, "Do you have any plans for lunch the day after tomorrow?"

"I sure hope I'm about to!"

The night finished on the best of notes: a peal of laughter.

•   •   •

The next day, I signed a month-to-month rental agreement for a houseboat just west of Lake Union. Then, even though it came furnished with little square-footage to spare, I bought the darn coffee table.

•   •   •

I must have changed five times in the shower trying to pick just the right outfit for what surely counted as our second date. Glamour was easier than clothes shopping, but I also liked that I could reserve the possibility of jumping into the sea if the date wasn't going well. Or would that be The Cut? Salmon Bay? I was still getting my bearings, but in any case ... jumping in the water without my natural coat would just make me a wet human.

I usually tried to keep my outfits simple, with loose-able accessories strictly off the rack and "off the glamour"—it would be a terribly vain downfall to be stuck on land forever because you glamoured up just the right scarf only to leave it behind.

The very nature of the clothes we wore made intimacy all the more vulnerable for selkies. To strip off one's coat with a lover required a huge amount of trust. I had never had that kind of relationship. Most of the sea lions in San Francisco had a leather-on policy. The clothes we shift into could be as revealing as we dreamed up, as long as they contained some piece of leather to anchor the glamour. I wondered where Tim wore his leather. I'd once reduced my coat to a single leather cuff, but that had been for someone who broke my heart. I fought back the sting of excess saline. He was nearly a thousand mile swim from here; I needed to stop letting him hurt me.

Any worry I'd had over wearing or doing the right thing melted away the moment I saw Tim's giant grin. He'd borrowed a picnic basket from one of his shipmates (she and her wife had a place in Fremont) and packed us a lunch to enjoy at Gasworks Park. We spent hours there, just talking and laughing in the sunshine, before strolling over to the shipyard where *Josephine Kelpie* was on the hard so I could see Tim's Alaska home.

Next stop, with only a brief mix-up over which bridge we should be looking under, was to visit the Fremont Troll

"I met someone who knew the model," I confessed.

Tim put his hand on my arm and leaned into me as he laughed, then he looked into my eyes with a strange sort of seriousness.

"Kautak? Can I kiss you?"

I barely stifled a moan of relief. "Please!"

Our kiss was delayed only briefly by laughter.

•   •   •

I brought Tim back to my place. He laughed at my double decker coffee table, the new acquisition stacked on top of the one that came with the boat because there was nowhere else to put it. The only piece of furniture we needed that night was the bed.

A not entirely pleasant adrenaline kicked in as our clothes started to come off because, of course, they weren't just clothes. I was letting this man peel my skin away. It wasn't painful, but it was terrifying the way I imagined skydiving must be. The gravitational pull of this moment was already working away at my layers. I couldn't just pop in the shower and change. No, that wasn't true. I was confident that Tim would respectfully halt everything that was happening if I pumped the brakes. I just didn't want to. I wanted to let this riptide drag me away from all my lubber insecurities.

•   •   •

The next morning, I awoke to find myself naked in a way I'd never been before, and yet wrapped in a warmth my selkie coat had never provided. We spent the entire, beautiful day together. We rented a rowboat from a little maritime museum at the south end of Lake Union. We had afternoon coffee at an old firehouse then climbed to the best viewpoints in Queen Anne. We watched mongers throw fish around a market and I almost caught one in my teeth, which made Tim laugh so hard he snorted and some kid thought the pig statue had come to life. We watched the sunset whisper something to Mt. Rainier that made her blush.

Ignoring the posted hours, we strolled vaguely in the direction of home through Myrtle Edwards Park. For the umpteenth time, I hinted it would be a lovely spot for a swim. Then, tired of dropping hints, I kicked off my boots and started pulling off one Starry Night sock.

"Wait, I thought you were kidding. You can't go in there, man. You'll get hypothermia in minutes."

"I'll. Be. Fine." I flapped my coat to help emphasize my meaning. Tim looked nonplussed, then a little scared.

"Shit," he swore under his breath, then tried to puff himself up. "Look, I think we had some kind of misunderstanding. Have a good night, Kautak. I'm heading home."

"Hold on, are you ..." I began. Tim looked like he really didn't want to stick around, but gave me one last chance to play it off as a joke. I didn't. "Are you really not a selkie?"

He looked devastated. "Is there ... someone I can call for you? Someone who helps when, um, you're like this?"

The poor man thought I was crazy, but despite his fear was sweet enough to stick around and find me help. Just when I didn't think I could fall harder for this guy, I did. And I was about to lose him, and my heart was cracking like a salmon's skull under my molars.

"I'm going to get disowned for this," I groaned as I stepped backwards into Elliott Bay.

"No, wait! We can find help from someone else; it doesn't have to be family. It'll be OK." Tim reached out in a panic. He probably thought I was about to drown myself in my sorrows.

Only the kind of drowning that involves malted grains, my friend, and only if this doesn't work.

I took one more step back, and shifted.

Usually I close my eyes for the transition, otherwise the warping, rolling sensation gets to my stomach like reading on a bus, but I couldn't tear my eyes from Tim. His eyes glazed over for a moment, unfocused and confused by the lens of glamour, but then he saw me. His jaw dropped, then his whole body sank to the damp grass. Already forgetting I was in my sea lion form, I surged forward to help him and was met by a terrified yell. I eased myself into the water so I could shift back.

Tim seemed, if anything, *more* horrified once I was human again. I turned red as a cucumber when I realized why.

I'd neglected to concentrate on a specific glamour for my coat as I stepped out of Elliott Bay. Instead of the bomber jacket I'd walked in with, my poor little hungry heart cooked up the most over-the-top leather daddy ensemble I had ever worn.

"Ehhh ... I'm sorry, I'm sorry, I'll change," I babbled. This seemed to snap Tim out of his shock, because he marched right up to me and took my face in his hands.

"No one is asking you to change."

I didn't know if he was talking about my outfit or my whole self, but at that moment I didn't care because he was kissing me. He was kissing me and he tasted like rockfish tacos and he smelled like wool and brine and human.

I couldn't believe I'd fallen for a full-time human.

ONE YEAR LATER

I slipped into my sealion form well before sunrise and set out to find *Josephine Kelpie* as she cruised down Puget Sound. I'd been following the progress of Mortimer Crewe and his shipmates on my phone thanks to an app that tracked their ship's AIS. I don't know how old fishwives did it before modern technology, or without the ability to swim out into frigid waters for an early welcome.

Tim didn't toss me fish like rose petals the way he said he would, but we'd both known he was joking about that. The fish had been sold off in Alaska before the return voyage, and I could catch myself something far fresher. Tim did blow me a kiss, though, when he saw me sailing one long flipper out of the water. Real sea lions wouldn't be cooling off like that at night. I like to think Tim would have recognized me anyway.

Long distance was hard. A call from his satphone was no replacement for having Tim's fluffy warm body next to mine, but these long stretches apart made me hopeful we'd never feel complacent about our time together. More importantly, I was able to return to my family in California whenever he left for Alaska so neither of us felt like we'd had to give up something for our partner. Neither of us had to change.

It was an agonizing wait for *Josephine Kelpie* to be officially put to bed and Tim's shore leave to begin, but every bit of nervous tension that had accumulated during those hours immediately melted away when I could cradle Tim's adorable, pudgy, freckled, grinning face between my hands.

"I missed you too, Kautak," Tim said, chuckling. I kissed him, and we smelled of leather and wool and the sea.

FIXER UPPER

Helen Weil

THERE ISN'T MUCH LEFT OF ME by the time I arrive. A lot of me stayed in the hometown I left behind, and I feel paper-thin as I stand in the early morning sunlight.

The house—my house—is just as bad as the pictures online made it seem. An overgrown lawn chock full of weeds, grimey windows, peeling paint on the sidings. And yet, I love it. It's mine, after all. The first thing I can call *just mine*. How could I not love it immediately?

I trample a path through the weeds up to the front door and find that I have to jiggle the key, up and down then left and right, before it turns.

A stale, mildew scent hits me when I get inside. Light shines faintly through the windows, illuminating stained carpets and the tarp-covered furniture atop them. A layer of dust covers everything, just waiting to be kicked up.

It's a lot of work. But every good thing in life is.

• • •

My first day in my new home, I clean the kitchen. I scrub it top to bottom, and when I'm satisfied, I plug in the ancient refrigerator and listen to it hum. It's the first sound to occupy space. That night, I get dinner at a local 24-hour diner and listen to the townsfolk's conversations. No one bats an eye at the newcomer. I'm not sure if that means I've slipped seamlessly into their ranks, or if I'm an invisible observer.

In my hometown, I was always the latter. I spent my whole childhood there and didn't manage to make more of an impression than any of the innumerable tourists that came through in summer for the tulip festival. I don't think anyone noticed when I packed up and left. My childhood home was sold to a perfect nuclear family who fit into the town like a puzzle piece, and I faded away like the ghost I'd been playing my whole life.

Here, in this new town a thousand miles away, I don't want to be invisible. But sitting here in the diner, patrons moving around me like I'm just another fixture alongside the vinyl booths and chrome paneling, I'm not sure if I have a choice in the matter.

My first night as a homeowner, I sleep on the kitchen floor in a sleeping bag. A shadeless lamp I took from the living room shines on the kitchen counter. I remind myself that this is good enough for me, that I can be happy here. But the shadows are long, and sleep does not come easily.

•   •   •

All things look better in the daylight, including this house. My next task is pushing the old couch and recliners into the garage and scrubbing at the living room carpet until my arms ache. Some stains lift and others don't, but the lemony smell of the cleaner is better than stale carpet, so I consider it a win.

While taking a break from cleaning, I find a crank radio in the entryway closet and set it on the windowsill. It just barely catches the broadcast from a college in the city, but it's better than the local stuff.

I don't stop until the sun, low on the horizon, begins to come through the open windows in shades of fiery red. I go sit on my porch to cool down, and the cicadas and grasshoppers sing for me. Somewhere, a guitar is being played. I sit very still and listen. The guitarist goes over the same chorus nearly a dozen times, never without a sour note or two. To me, it sounds like a symphony.

A while later, the music stops and my neighbor's upstairs window on the second floor slides shut. In the low evening light, I think I see the shape of a man behind the curtain, but he's gone before I can make him out.

Again, I get food from the diner and sleep on the kitchen floor. I drift off a lot quicker tonight.

•   •   •

The third day, I try to finish the living room. The heavy, dust-coated curtains are left on the curb for the garbage collectors, and the windows are scrubbed with rag after rag. I only have a few windows done when I have to take a break to clean all of the rags in the kitchen sink. Brown water swirls down the drain. I wonder how many years it's been since sunlight was able to reach into this house.

In the living room, the little radio plays a staticy rendition of an old Twenty One Pilots song, and I take a deep breath before leaving the kitchen.

My grandma used to tell me that there weren't many problems that music couldn't make at least a little bit better. After a bad day, she would let me root through her vinyl collection and pick out the evening's soundtrack. Then, we would stand side by side in the kitchen, singing along to the music while we prepared dinner. Meals tasted better when we made them together.

After I finish the windows, I go outside to my trailer hitch and take out all the boxes labeled 'kitchen.' I'm carrying them inside in a precarious stack when I catch a glimpse of my neighbor in the upstairs window. This time I make out a face, though I can't tell what expression he's wearing. He retreats back from the window before I can wave.

The kitchen is finally usable, so I clean myself up and go into town to buy some groceries. While I'm walking the aisles and filling my basket, my thoughts drift back to my mysterious neighbor. I'm reminded of advice from my grandma: if you want to make a good impression on someone, make them cookies. So flour, eggs, sugar, butter, vanilla, and chocolate chips come home with me, too. It's the best dinner I've had in ages, and when I lay down in my sleeping bag, a fresh plate of chocolate chip cookies waits on the counter.

•   •   •

In the morning, I brave going upstairs to open up all of those windows and start airing everything out. I cover most of the master bathroom in bleach and go back downstairs with burning lungs. I pick up the plate of cookies and create a new path across my front yard over to my neighbor's.

The house is cookie-cutter perfect, like every other one on this block. Robin's egg blue, white shutters, a porch swing, and a maple tree.

Mine must have looked like this, once upon a time. I don't know why each of the houses on this block seem to have not changed since the day they were built while mine has been worn down harshly by time.

Maybe my neighbor can give me some answers. I knock, and it echoes down the quiet, empty street. A curtain flutters upstairs, and a minute later, the front door opens. A man stands at the threshold. To my surprise, he looks to be around my age.

I hold out the plate. "Hi. I'm Eve. I just moved in next door. Cookies?"

He blinks at me owlishly. "Sure," he says. "Thanks. I'm Max. It's nice to put a face to your voice. I always hear you singing along to your radio."

I feel my face begin to grow warm. "Sorry, I'll turn it down."

"No, don't worry about it. I like the music. It's pretty quiet out here."

"You've got that right." The street behind me is empty; it's a Sunday morning and there are no children playing, lawns being mowed, sprinklers spraying. It's totally dead. It's like we're the only two people left in the world.

"Well, I have to get back to work," he says. "But feel free to stop by anytime. Especially if you have cookies with you."

This drags a smile out of me for the first time in a very long time. "You got it, Max."

"See you around, Eve."

The door closes with a soft click, and I'm alone again.

•   •   •

I don't see Max again until after I've finished cleaning the whole first floor of my house, but I hear him play his guitar almost every night. I upgrade from a sleeping bag to a mattress and make the barren living room my new bedroom. When I open the window, I can hear him perfectly. Sometimes, he even sings along, slow Spanish songs that remind me of the stuff my grandma had on vinyl. I fall asleep to it more than once.

Before I tackle the second floor of my house, I decide to fix the neglected front yard. It's wild and unsightly, and burrs stick to my shoes every time I have to trek through it.

I don't have a lawnmower, and I certainly don't have the funds to buy one. So I walk over to Max's house and knock on the door, fingers crossed at my side. The sun is low in the sky and warms the back of my neck. I had busied myself with sweeping up cobwebs in the garage until the afternoon sun stopped beating down so ferociously, but the air is still oppressively hot.

Max answers the door quicker today than the last time I knocked.

"Eve," he says, sounding surprised. He's wearing an apron, a frilly one my grandma would like, and I can hear something sizzling down the hall in the kitchen. With a start, I realize that his house is laid out identically to mine. I should have expected that. They are—or were once—identical on the outside; why wouldn't they be identical on the inside?

"Do you have a lawnmower I can borrow?" I ask.

He raises his eyebrows at me. "Sure. Give me ten and I can bring it over."

For ten long minutes, I use a rusty shovel I found in the garage to chip away at the earth spilling over onto the sidewalk, trying to at least figure out where the stones end and the lawn begins. When Max's garage door begins to open, the sound is so jarring against the peaceful summer sounds that I jump. Max emerges, no longer wearing his apron, pushing a red lawnmower in front of him.

"Thank you," I say. "This is driving me crazy."

He shrugs. "No problem. I've got a weedwacker, too, if you're feeling ambitious."

"Maybe tomorrow," I say, hoping to sound nonchalant. Really, I have no idea how to use one.

His curious eyes see right through me. "You don't know how to use a weed wacker, do you?"

"Was it obvious?"

He laughs. "Yeah, the deer in headlights look gave you away."

I find myself laughing, too. I'm surprised at how easily it comes back to me.

"Well, I can help you if you want," he says. "I've got nothing to do tomorrow."

I wave away his offer. "I don't want to make you—"

"You're not making me do anything. I'd love to help."

I look at his eyes, wide and brown and earnest, and I trust that he's telling the truth. My grandma used to say I was good at reading people. It's all in the eyes. They say everything.

"Okay. I'll make you more cookies as payment," I tell him.

"Deal." He sticks out a hand to shake, and I take it. It's warm and calloused and strong. After, my hand buzzes from the casual touch.

He heads back to his house, and I start cutting down the forest that has taken over my yard. Despite the difficult labor, I'm fighting a smile the whole time.

•　　　•　　　•

Max knocks on my door at exactly ten o'clock the next morning. The cookie dough is still sitting in the mixing bowl.

"Good morning," he says. "I hope it isn't too early."

"No, it's fine. The cookies aren't done, though."

He leans the weedwacker against the siding. "How can I help?"

"I just have to put them in the oven," I say. "But you can come in while you wait."

I hold open the door for him and he follows me inside. I see my house through his eyes. It's not dirty, but it's practically empty and still needs a lot of work. My face heats up and I hurry him to the kitchen.

"This place looks great," he says, surveying the kitchen.

The kitchen is definitely the part of the house that's in the best shape, but the backsplash behind the sink is outdated and the cabinet doors are faded and the appliances are a little rusted. Under my sneaker, a tile is cracked in half, and there are many more like it around us. "It's functional. Still has a long way to go before 'great.'"

Max puts a hand on my arm, stopping me in the middle of rolling a dough ball between my hands. "Eve, you should be proud of yourself. Before you moved in, I thought this place was way beyond saving. But here you are, working miracles."

Now my face is warm for another reason. "I'm not a miracle worker. Just making the best of what I could afford."

He offers no rebuttal, and we fall into comfortable silence while I work. The oven pings and groans as it warms up. He walks to the windowsill, where the old radio is sitting, and winds the hand crank with ease.

"How long have you lived here?" I ask.

"The house, a couple years. But I've lived in this town my whole life."

"Did you know the people who owned this house before me?"

"No," he says. "It was already abandoned by the time I was a teenager."

I slide the trays of cookies into the oven and slam the creaky door, then wind up a timer. "Okay, ready."

We make quick work of the yard, him trimming a neat line around the edges of the overgrown lawn and me following behind with a shovel to clear off the walkway. He continues to cut at the weeds pressing against the siding while I go inside to get the cookies, and I come back outside with a plate and a pitcher just as he's finishing up. We both gulp down ice water like we've never been more parched.

"Can you make me these every day?" he says. "I think they're the best things I've ever had."

"If you keep helping me with this house, I'll make you cookies any time you ask," I joke.

He turns to me with an expression that's more serious than I expected. "Deal."

"Oh," I say. "Sure."

Max goes home soon after, and I go back to cleaning the second floor. Most of the furniture is too heavy to move, but I suppose I can just wait for Max to help me move them.

The rest of my day is taken up with working on another bathroom. I clean the windows and mirror until they sparkle, scrub and recaulk the bathtub, and polish the faucets. Mopping isn't enough to get the floor clean, so I end up on my hands and knees, scrubbing between the floor tiles with a toothbrush I dipped in bleach, and I don't stop until my head starts to spin from the fumes.

When I retire to my living room mattress that night, Max is playing his guitar in his bedroom. He must know I can hear him. I choose to believe he's playing for me.

•   •   •

Max shows up on my doorstep the next morning in paint-splattered jeans and the rattiest t-shirt I've ever seen.

"You were serious," I say.

"Good morning," he says. "I was."

"Okay, then. I need some help getting the old furniture down from the second floor. You want some coffee first?"

"I'd love some," he says.

He takes his with milk and sugar. I take mine black. We sit together on the kitchen counter, our feet swinging like we're children.

"Where are you from?" he says. "I didn't ask yesterday."

"The coast," I tell him. "I grew up in a town so small there's no way you've heard of it."

"Try me."

"Duneland Beach."

He nods, contemplative.

"You've never heard of it," I say.

"I have! It's, uh, you know ... by the coast."

We break down into laughter. It really wasn't funny, but I'm drunk on happiness, and I think he might be, too. Our coffee mugs sit forgotten on the counter, twin threads of steam rising in the golden sunlight.

·　　　·　　　·

"Why did you leave?" he asks while we're carrying a ridiculously big armoire down the stairs.

"What?"

"The coast," he says between strained breaths. He's taking the brunt of the weight; I'm just making sure it doesn't fall on him. "Why'd you leave?"

"Needed a change," I say. "Hey, watch that corner."

I don't tell him about my grandma and how the house by the water felt too big without her in it. He doesn't ask. Instead, we begin to talk about the desks we remove from the three bedrooms.

"The maiden of the house, a stately woman named Clara with a melancholic streak, would use it to write in her diary nightly," I propose.

"How old do you think this house is?" he asks.

I look him dead in the eyes and say, "Ancient."

He rolls his eyes and hoists the desk a little higher. "It was built in the '60s. They all were."

"Really?"

"Yeah, some architect thought he would get rich off white flight bringing everyone out here to the boonies, so he bought this big empty chunk of land and built rows of cookie-cutter houses. I think this neighborhood was pretty lively back then, but no one really lives out here now, except us and some snowbirds that won't let go of their houses."

"Hang on." We drop the desk at the foot of the stairs. "Why was this one left to rot? Why did you move here if it's empty? I'm so confused."

Max regards me for a minute with eyes the color of a starless night. "Tomorrow," he says. "Come over for dinner, and I'll tell you everything I know."

"Oh," I say. "Okay."

"It's a date," he says, then he picks up the desk and carries it the rest of the way to the garage, leaving me reeling on the landing.

Long after Max goes home, my head continues to spin. He's the first person to meet the version of me untethered from a past I dragged around like a ball and chains. I was so wrapped up in it I could hardly breathe. I'm still getting used to being free.

I don't really know this new Eve yet. I wonder what Max sees in her.

•   •   •

I fall asleep much later than usual and wake to midmorning sunlight pouring through my windows. Now that the upstairs has been cleared out, I can begin to clean the bedrooms. I move room to room, clearing cobwebs, thick and gray from years of dust, from nearly every corner. My mind is miles away in a beach house occupied by a girl and her grandmother.

My grandmother used to make fun of people who said the world was as unpredictable as the tides. If you know the ocean, she would say, you would know that the tides are as predictable as the rise and set of the sun. As predictable as the seasons that bring the tourists and send them away. The world, she would say, is much more unpredictable.

Two decades ago, my parents met, fell in love, got married, and bought a house on the beach. They had me. The tides ebbed and flowed. The sun rose and set. The seasons changed. Predictable.

One night, my parents didn't make it home. An accident, the hospital said. Unpredictable. But the tides continued to ebb and flow, the sun continued to rise and set, and the seasons changed. My grandmother raised me, and we were happy, for the most part. I grew up, and she aged. Shortly after my twentieth birthday, she went to sleep and didn't wake up. Predictable, I suppose. Just not to me.

After that, the beach house was too big, too haunted, for just me. I started to fade away, too. I had to let it go.

This new house is better. It's smaller, perfect for just one. The ghosts I left in the sprawling beach house couldn't follow me here.

•   •   •

It's nice to have a friend who lives so close. He told me to come over at six o'clock, which meant I didn't have to leave my house until exactly six o'clock. However, waiting was torturous. After clearing the cobwebs, I clean all of the windows on the second floor, and I still have time to bake cookies. I sit on the floor as they bake, watching the dough puff up and counting the seconds as they pass.

But standing in front of his door, a plate of cookies in hand and the sun warm on my back, I wish there had been a little bit more time before I had to walk over. His words, "it's a date," ring in my ears.

The door is open, and I can hear him cooking in the kitchen. It smells like spices and reminds me of the comfort of a home-cooked meal. I knock, and he shouts that I can come in. I take my time walking down the hallway, savoring a version of my house that time was kinder to. I find Max with a towel over his shoulder, standing over a pan of popping oil.

"So," I say. "You owe me a story."

"I do," he says, "but pasta first."

So we have pasta. It tastes like good company. Max tells me about growing up in this town—summers spent wandering the woods, buying his first guitar second-hand with his meager allowance, getting pancakes from the diner after prom, leaving for college and being so homesick he moved back the day after graduation.

"You love it here," I say.

He picks up his wine glass, twirling it between his fingers. "I do. It's home, you know? No place like it."

I think of my home. A beach. A too-big house. My grandmother's warm smile. A simple truth comes to light: I miss it, but not enough to go back.

Another truth springs up beside it: I like it here. I like the work of fixing up my house. I like spending time with Max. I like the quiet. I like the life I'm making for myself.

"So what about you?" he asks. "Do you miss home?"

"No," I say. "It's right here."

He raises his glass, and we toast to home.

•   •   •

I help him clean up after dinner, and by the time we're done, the stifling evening heat has relaxed into a warm, breezy night. We take my plate of cookies—snickerdoodles this time—out to the porch and sit under the heavy blanket of stars.

"They're so clear out here," he says. "Can't get that in the city."

"I've never lived in a city. I've always known a sky full of stars," I say.

"Count yourself lucky. There's really nothing better."

I look over at Max. He's leaning back on his elbows, head tilted up to the sky. His dark eyes reflect the dim light of a nearby streetlamp.

"Yeah, I am pretty lucky," I say.

His gaze slides over to me, and I don't look away. It feels like we're the only two people in the world, but it isn't lonely. He reaches for me and I for him, and the bright stars above us fade away.

•   •   •

I wake up early to rain tapping on my windows. Thunder rumbles in the distance. I keep the radio's volume low, barely more than a whisper of static, and I take my time ripping the sun-faded carpet out of each bedroom. When it's all done, strips of carpet arranged in neat rolls at the top of the stairs, I open one of the windows and throw them out onto the lawn, soaking my arms and the windowsill in the process. It feels good on my overheated skin.

When the pile is gone, I close the window, throw a towel down over the puddle, and go outside. I stand on the sidewalk, face turned up to meet the falling rain. Water streams over my cheeks and into my ears, but I don't miss the sound of a door opening.

I turn and watch as Max opens an umbrella and starts cutting across our front yards.

"Need some help?" he asks, gesturing with his free hand to the piles of carpet on the lawn.

"Yes," I say. I take the umbrella from his hand and toss it to the side. I kiss him, my thumbs tracing the raindrops' path over his cheekbones, and his hands find my hips. The way my cold, wet shirt sticks to my skin is uncomfortable, but Max is warm and steady against me.

When I pull away, he stares at me like he's seeing me for the first time.

"What?" I ask.

"Nothing." Rain clings to his eyelashes, darkening them. He lets go of me to rub a hand over his face. "So, do you actually want help with the trash or can we go inside?"

"Don't tell me you're afraid of a little water," I say, thinking of how the bottoms of my pants were always wet when I was growing up. I would wade into the shallows every day after school. When I got older, I learned to love a late-night walk when the water was glass-still, a mirror image of the stars above it.

"No," he says, "but I would have put on my swimsuit if I knew we were going to be recreating *The Notebook*."

I roll my eyes. "Come on, then. We'll be quick."

We stack the rolls of carpet by the street, and Max invites himself over for coffee. "It's the least you could do, making me work in the rain."

"You're the one who chose to walk over," I remind him, but I find him a towel and start the coffee maker anyways.

He looks around appraisingly as he rubs the towel over his wet curls. "Looking better every day, Eve," he says.

I shake my head. "There's still so much to do. I've barely started."

"I think everyone feels that way when they own a house. You get used to it."

I take two mugs out of the cabinet and pour our coffee. I make one with milk and sugar and pass it to him. He hops up onto my counter, and I follow suit.

"You know, I realized I did know the person who owned this house," he says. "I mean, I met him once. This place *was* abandoned when I was a kid, but someone did still technically own it. I guess the deed to the property had been put in a trust and left to the owners' son when they died. Late last year, he came by a couple times to check it out, and he said he was abroad when they passed and he didn't know about the house being left to him. I don't know, I never got the whole story. Around Christmas time, he stopped showing up and the 'for sale' sign went up. Guess he decided it wasn't worth keeping."

"Is it bad that I'm glad he didn't keep it?"

"I don't think so," Max says. "Maybe he knew someone was going to come around who would love it more than he did."

I think about my childhood home and the new family living in it, enjoying every day on the beach like my grandmother and I once did. I loved it so much, and I think that they'll love it more than I did.

"Do you ever regret staying here?" I ask. "It seems like it can get lonely."

"Not at all. I might not have many neighbors in the warmer months, but the crickets and the cicadas keep me company. And now you." He puts an arm around me, pulling me a little bit closer. "The world isn't empty, even when it feels like it."

•　　　•　　　•

Little by little, my house starts to come back to life. Once I'm no longer scared of stepping on splinters or stray staples, I start sleeping in the primary bedroom. I hang up my clothes in the closet, and the stack of boxes in the trailer starts to dwindle. I even buy a bedframe and a mattress, and Max helps me put it all together. He starts staying over some nights, and I stay over at his house other times.

Little by little, the seasons change. Towards the end of summer, I find someone to paint the house a pale yellow. It looks great next to Max's pale blue.

In the fall, a few of our neighbors return. Max introduces me to all of them, and I never show up without a plate of cookies.

In the winter, the neighborhood is full again. I get a job at the diner. People start to know my name, and I start to know theirs. Max and I go Christmas tree shopping, and we fall asleep together on his couch after decorating his tree. The next morning, we decorate mine. One of the older couples in our neighborhood invites us to a party on the 26th, and Max and I go together.

In the spring, I plant rose bushes in my front yard, and they bloom in vibrant red and pink. Every time I open the windows, the smell reminds me of my grandma.

In the summer, I take Max to the coast, to see a place where the summer brings people in instead of sending them away. I tell him about my parents and my grandma, and he brings flowers to the cemetery. Pink and red roses.

The tide ebbs and flows. The sun rises and sets. Max stays by my side, and the world is never empty.

WHERE I BELONG

Bianca M. Bispo

S HE LOVED WATCHING HIM. The quickness of his breath, the strategic gliding of his eyes across the field as he locked upon his target and kicked. The ball flew through the air, the crowd quieted and she could feel the weight of it in her throat as she held her breath. The ball soared past the goalie, right into the net. The stadium erupted, a laugh tore through her before she leapt and cheered. She saw his teammates pile onto him before he broke free and pointed at her with unrestricted joy spread across his face.

She could still remember the first time she saw him. She was waiting for the bus outside the university's football field. The sun had set long ago and yet she was still on campus since her new position as a journalist for the university's student magazine had her attending late meetings and tiresome conferences. There came a group of voices to her left and there he was, in the midst of a gaggle of boys with his duffel bag slung over his shoulder, chatting absentmindedly. He caught her eye and grinned. She whipped her head away. The bus whined to a stop in front of them and Carmen sat at the back in the seat closest to the window. She heard him before she saw him, boisterously chatting even in the quietness of the nearly vacant bus. She rolled her eyes, put on her headphones and tuned them out.

The weeks passed and another brain-numbing meeting took place. The categories were written on the board again: arts, global news, politics, and on it went.

"Now," said Daniel, the editor-in-chief, "Peyton usually covers sports, but he's sick and won't be able to do it this week so I need someone to take his place."

Usually, Carmen would flock to the political column, but she knew the popularity the sports articles had amongst readers and she was tired of having her articles be buried as an afterthought within the later pages. That was why, despite her inexperience, she raised her hand.

"I'd like to do it."

Daniel nodded and wrote her name on the board. A few others volunteered and the meeting ended with Daniel announcing the decision would be made by the end of the week with an email sent to the chosen author. Again, Carmen gathered her things and waited for the bus at the stop next to the football field. Again, the voices approached the bus stop and again, there he was, laughing amongst his friends. And again, their eyes met. And again, Carmen moved her gaze away from him.

The email appeared in her inbox a little less than two days later. She was chosen for the sports column. There was a soccer game on Saturday whose team was the pride and joy of the university and Carmen made sure to get tickets.

She had never been much of a sports fan, but there was something sacred about soccer. Perhaps it was because of her father and his love for the sport, but soccer managed to ignite a passion within her. Adrenaline already thundered within her as she made her way to her seat. The crowd cheered, holding up merchandise as the players entered the arena. Carmen had brought her notebook with her and as the game went on, she made notes on the faults, the passes, the goals. Still, she found her eyes wandering to the player with the number eight on his back. His passes, his yells, his hunger as he carried the counterattack.

The ball rolled violently across the grass, assisted by gentle touches as it neared the net. With a furious kick, the ball scraped the fingertips of the goalie and flew into the goal. The crowd roared, the game was finished. They had won three to one.

Carmen waited outside the dressing room and there he was, with his back against the wall talking to his coach. The other players filed past her and every passing second revived her adrenaline until impatience started to thrum within her. When the conversation ended, his eyes found hers, his eyebrow quirking up.

"I'd like to interview you for the university magazine." The words rushed out of her before she could rethink them.

"Peyton usually interviews," he questioned.

"I'm filling in for him," Carmen clarified, "and I'd like to interview you."

"Now?"

"Now."

He led her to the empty bleachers and she flipped open her notebook. She pressed record on a new voice memo and placed her phone between them.

"Could you state your name and position for the record?" She asked. Without the crowd, her voice seemed to float across the stadium. The floodlights still shone, illuminating them.

He leaned forward so he was right above the phone. "Andrew Lawler, striker."

"Thank you. Now, you assisted two goals and scored the last one yourself. You clearly had a lot of strategic passes leading up to those moments. How were you able to create those strategies?"

"It's all a matter of following the gameplay and improvising when the time is right." The words flowed out of him as if rehearsed as he leaned back on the heels of his palms. "My teammates made it easier for me, of course, by improvising along with me and passing to me. I don't think I should take all the credit for that."

She hummed, amused. "How humble of you."

He shrugged, a smile tugging at his mouth. "I try."

"It was a big win! How do you celebrate after a win like that?"

"Well, usually the guys like to go out for pizza, but maybe I'll do something different this time."

She scribbled in her notebook. "Oh, yeah? Like what?"

"Maybe I'll ask you to continue this interview over dinner. With me."

Carmen stopped. Looked up. He was grinning at her, leaning forwards and patiently awaiting her answer. She let out a laugh.

"I have to be home in an hour," she told him. She stopped recording and started packing up her things. He watched silently until she stood there with her bag slung over her shoulder, staring down at him.

"Is that ... a yes, then?" He asked.

"Depends." She smiled. "Where are we going?"

The restaurant was nearly empty, considering that it was relatively late and most students had already gone home. Still, some had decided to have dinner on campus and a few tables hosted couples and singles alike. It was a small, dimly lit Italian place with linen tablecloths and candlelit tables. They sat next to the window, Carmen taking the booth while Andrew sat in the chair facing her. It was dark enough that Carmen could see her reflection in the window, the low restaurant lights bright against the navy blue blanketing the campus. The waitress brought them breadsticks and water while they perused the menu. When they had ordered, Carmen took out her pen and notebook and laid her phone between them. He sat with his arms crossed over the table. As it shook gently, utensils clinking softly against one another, Carmen realized his leg was restlessly bouncing underneath it.

"Nervous?" She joked.

He laughed and through the cracks of the sound, she could tell that he was. She bit back a smile and turned her attention to her notebook. She clicked her pen twice, a nervous tick of her own.

"To pick up where we left off, the Hawks are a treasured team here—the pride of the school, some might say," she began. The table stopped shaking as he watched her with amusement dancing in his eyes. She cleared her throat and continued, "Would you say the pressure affects you and your performance?"

He looked down at his breadstick and was quiet for a moment, long enough where Carmen asked herself if she should take back the question.

Eventually, he spoke. "It's hard for it not to affect me. I wish I could say it doesn't, but it's something I think about constantly, honestly. I try not to let it affect my performance, though, since I don't want to get too fixed on it, but it's always there, looming over me. I mean, I have a lot at risk. There's my scholarship, for one, and my future in sports. I don't want to give any of that up."

Carmen began to write when Andrew stopped her.

"Could you leave out the part about, you know, me having a lot at stake?" He asked.

"Why? I mean, the readers might resonate with it; it'll make them root for you."

He grimaced. She caught it and nodded, crossing out the bullet-point she'd written.

"Okay. Consider it gone."

"Now, I'm curious about you," Andrew said, spearing a piece of chicken with his fork. "You've already asked so much about me, but I don't even know your name."

Carmen smiled to herself. She liked being anonymous during interviews as she noticed it usually gave her more professional answers rather than a false sense of camaraderie that inevitably leaked into her articles, but, somehow, she didn't mind sharing this time.

"Carmen," she said. Then, lightheartedly, jokingly, "nice to meet you."

He smiled. "Nice to meet you, Carmen."

As it turned out, Andrew lived only a few blocks away from her and accompanied her on her ride home. She found him to be very witty, extroverted and, well, handsome. She watched as the dark color of his hair reflected the yellow streetlights and how the shadows split across his jaw. There was a certain familiarity about him that went beyond friendliness, an aspect of him that made it easy for her to converse with him as if they'd known each other for decades. She found herself wishing the night could drag on and the bus would never reach her house.

"Let me know when you start writing the article," he said as they stood where their paths split. "I'd love to help you out."

"Will do."

He smiled once more and waved before walking down the small hill. She watched him for a few seconds before walking home.

Their meetings became more frequent as the days went on. Sometimes, she would unintentionally meet him at the bus stop after a meeting, other times she would intentionally wait for him outside the stadium, but her favourite times were when he messaged her and waited for her outside her classes. Their chats in coffee shops eventually turned into sneaking into empty classrooms and kissing under the bleachers. Through it all, Carmen's heart thrummed with adrenaline and fondness whenever she locked eyes with him. During a specific soccer practice, he had worn a black muscle tank that made her so flustered, she barely looked at him.

"You know you haven't properly looked at me this whole time, right?" He said as they walked toward the bus stop. "What's up with you?"

She mumbled something incoherent against the palm of her hand and he took it away from her mouth, fingers intertwining with hers.

"Sorry, what was that?" He asked.

"It's your shirt," she said.

"What about my shirt?" He frowned, looking down at it. Then, after a moment, a shit-eating grin broke across his face. "Oh, is it doing something for you, Carmie?"

Carmen simply mumbled an embarrassed "oh my god" before Andrew burst into laughter.

The next time they met was on the bleachers. Carmen was sitting with her computer open in her lap and her notebook open next to her. She had previously transcribed all the significant parts of their recorded conversation into rough paragraphs and was expanding them in her Word document when Andrew appeared next to her. She had heard the metal stands creak before he nudged her with the tip of his duffel bag and she turned to face him. He was wearing the black muscle tank she loved on him and she wondered if he had worn it for her. He grinned, wide and dimpled, when her eyes met his. He dropped his bag and sat next to her, peering at her computer screen.

"Need any help?" He asked.

She shook her head.

"Not yet," she told him, "but I might ask you to proofread it later."

He waited as she finished her first draft, eyes watching the empty field until she placed the computer in his lap. He smiled at her,, but it didn't reach his eyes. She had seen his face before she'd interrupted his staring, it had been strangely blank.

"Everything okay?" She asked, tilting her head. His smile fell and he pursed his lips.

"Just thinking," he said. When he didn't continue, she debated dropping the subject,, but he didn't move to distract her either, so she pressed it.

"About?"

"I'm not sure if I want to keep doing this," he said. He didn't look at her, his eyes were back on the field. "I'm not sure soccer is what I want to do anymore. I don't know, I'm slowly falling out of love with it." He looked at her then, a sheepish smile on his face. "Please don't tell anyone I said that."

She smiled kindly. "I won't ..., but I think you should know, people fall out of love with their craft all the time." She watched the field, the sun spread through the pines, rays reflecting off the metal bleachers. "I've asked myself so many times if I actually love journalism or if it's just something I'm doing because it's what I've always wanted to do. It's something I've wanted for so long, I'm not sure if it'll be everything I dreamed of once I finally get to do it professionally. Then, I think of what else I would rather do and there's nothing, absolutely nothing I want more and I know, that's where I belong."

He shifted closer to her and she rested her head on his shoulder as he edited her article.

"Do you really think it's good?" She asked sheepishly once he had handed her laptop back to her.

"It's brilliant," he said. There was a fondness in his voice that sent a wave of giddiness through her and she smiled into the palm of her hand.

That Friday, the article was published on the front page of the magazine, with a photo of Andrew running across the field, the winning ball at his feet. When they met after her last class, he had a copy of the magazine clutched in his hand as he hugged her tightly.

The whistle blew, the stadium thundered, and Andrew flew down the pitch. With the ball between his feet, he paused for a millisecond and in the stands, Carmen held her breath. He drew in a breath and the stadium froze in place as his foot kicked the ball into the air. The goalie dove, but came a split second short and the ball, gracefully and gently, rolled into the goal behind him. The stadium erupted and as Carmen jumped with glee, she knew what he had also come to realize, that was where he belonged.

WHEN WE SAY
NOTHING AT ALL

I.S.A. Crisostomo Lopez

MY MOTHER WAS A JOURNALIST, a senior correspondent for one of the largest newspapers in the city. My father was a musician and professor at the university. So I grew up breathing the dust that lay on books, journals, and magazines, and listening to classical piano pieces that evoke the deepest emotions. Classic novels of all kinds littered our cramped library while the spacious sala paid homage to a piano of dark polished wood.

I was very proud of my mother, especially when her name appeared in the papers. I would brag about her in school, showing off a newspaper item to my classmates, on how she had uncovered the biggest gambling scandal involving top officials of our municipality.

When my mother came out with that exposé, my father was enraged. They had previously agreed that she would give the story to a junior reporter, but I guess she just couldn't drop it. Like a treasure hunter, she couldn't let go of the shovel with the gold already glinting out of the ground.

My mother was fearless, brash and stubborn. She discounted the threats on her life, and just as quickly as the world was shocked with her exposé, we were stunned at how suddenly she was taken from us—succumbing to a single bullet in the head fired through her office window. I was 14-years-old then.

My father said that words printed on paper could make or unmake anyone. This was the reason why she was killed, he explained to me. We never found out who killed her. Without any incriminating evidence, the police failed to produce any suspects. Their investigation only led to one dead end after another. My father believed that the hitman must have really been paid well so as not to leave any trail. Either that or someone paid to mess with the investigation.

My mother's death left a void inside me. I would cry without understanding why. But it seemed my tears were lamentations for the loss of an idol rather than a mother. Like my mother, I also like writing down my thoughts in a journal. But in college, I pursued creative writing instead of journalism. Perhaps a part of me wanted to follow her footsteps, and another part wanted to be my own person.

As the days passed, I noticed how her absence took its toll upon my father. He grew weary and never recovered from the grief that had stricken his frail heart. He would read all the cards and love letters my mother had written to him in the past. He would take them out of their boxes, bundles of them, and read aloud words so wonderfully written by a woman to her man. He would sit at the piano and play her favorite love songs. He would play with passion, as if he were invoking her spirit to come back. But after four or five songs, he would stop. I wasn't sure why he would stop but I saw him misty-eyed, sullen, and suddenly gray-haired.

My father's been teaching at the university for as long as I can remember. He loves music and his job enables him to share it with others who are also passionate about it. But that flame burning within him seemed to burn less and less until it was completely extinguished.

Watching my father deteriorate each day was even more painful than my mother's sudden demise. He would force a dry smile at my occasional jokes, but his eyes showed no light, only shadows.

My father eventually passed away, leaving me the house, his piano, a garden full of cacti and our dog, Jacuzzi.

Still single and fresh out of university, I lived alone, wondering what life to lead. My aunts and uncles would occasionally visit me, sometimes allowing my cousins to sleep over on the weekends. It was fun, at least for the time being. We would stay up late, pigging out on root beer and fried potato fingers, watching old movies or simply talking about boyfriends—their boyfriends.

I hated to stand by the gate and see my cousins ride away in their car. I hated to see their heads looking back, their hands waving goodbye. I hated goodbyes. I hated people leaving. Sometimes I would ask God why people came into my life, only to leave me.

I inherited my mother's skill with words and my father's romantic heart for music. I accepted the invitation to teach Creative Writing at the university. Life was hard but I kept it simple, following a strict, neatly-written-down schedule of activities:

Wake up at 6:00 a.m.
Breakfast at 7:00 a.m.
Classes from 8:30 a.m. to 11:00 a.m.
Consultation hour from 11:00 a.m. to 12:00 noon
Lunch break from 12:00 noon to 1:30 p.m.
Consultation hour 1:30 p.m. to 2:30 p.m.
Classes from 3:00 p.m. to 5:00 p.m.

End of Day one. During weekends, I taught piano lessons at home to grade schoolers.

My friends kept pushing me to go out on dates, saying I must find someone who'll look after me. I already have my dog, I told them. Besides, dating is way out of my schedule.

When I reached my 28th birthday, my friends arranged a blind date for me, saying I must open myself to romantic possibilities. 'Possibilities' sounded logical, so I assented to one, just one. My friends clapped and hurrahed at my answer. At least, they felt their years-long efforts did not come to naught.

The date was set at Café Valerie which was near the theater so my date and I could have dinner and afterwards enjoy a musical ballet. (I love musical ballet! The ballerinas skittering on their toes always reminds me of the beauty of the human body, the majesty of art, and how every graceful movement seems to produce a tinkling sound undetected by the human ear but genuinely felt.)

I arrived at the place at 7:00 p.m. as agreed upon. Tables were starting to fill with young men spending time, waiting for the gala show. Their girlfriends were sipping iced coffee quietly, fingers busy fidgeting mobile phone keys. Everyone seemed to know how to escape the wait.

Thirty minutes passed. I looked down at my cup, surveying every minute detail to reduce my anxiety. I discovered the rim was not a perfect circle but oval like an egg. The shape of my teaspoon was oval, too. My cappuccino had lost its froth, save for its aroma still floating in the air. The bonsai plant that solely adorned my table was made of green plastic. Its pot was solid clay with intricate gold geometric design.

After an hour, the coffee shop was deserted with every customer departing to line up at the theater. The show must be starting in an hour or so.

The waiter behind the bar was putting away the glasses. Another waiter was mopping the floor. Since my date was a no-show, I decided to go home. Walking to the bus stop, I could still see the entire restaurant clearly etched in my mind, having spent one full hour staring at each nook.

After the foiled date, my friends finally left me alone. They stopped talking about dates. They felt ashamed for letting me wait for over an hour for someone who didn't have the nerve to show up or at least send a message of apology. But as days passed, they were back to their cheerful, hopeful selves that I'd find my soul mate without their intervention. But not without a stern reminder to keep watch for that magic spark, that x-factor which would signal that I have finally found Mr. Right, because if I don't keep my senses sharp enough, I might just miss it.

•   •   •

Fiction writing class. Second semester. I was giving the class some last pointers before their mid-term exams when I caught his eyes. A beautiful pair of tawny brown eyes. Striking. Marvelous. Astounding. Baffling. Seeking. Penetrating. Shimmering against the light of the fluorescent bulb hanging overhead. This young senior had the most beautiful eyes I have ever seen and he was looking at me. I hated the feeling it evoked like I was put under a spotlight. As a teacher, I felt I should be in command. So I resolved to take all his attention.

"Any questions, class? Do you want to say something, Mr. Consignado?"

His face lit up with a start but he was quick to respond. "Yes, I was hoping we could opt to take the exams in the afternoon instead? I'm with the basketball team and we have scheduled the whole morning for practice."

My womanly, motherly instinct wanted to say yes, of course. It's not a big deal. I understand. But my stubborn side was envious of basketball or any other preoccupation which says fiction writing isn't important at all and can take the backseat. So I said no. "Take the exams in the morning just like everybody else or see you next trimester. I don't give preferential treatment."

The next day, I found a note on my desk, a yellow-brown handmade paper with a neat scribble that said, "A break is all I ask." Signed, Nathaniel Consignado. Fiction writing class.

I wanted to crumple the paper and throw it in the nearest bin but the words written on it seemed to be ringing in my ear. I was motionless for a few moments as if listening to a fleeting melody. His words echoed a queer, inexplicable din.

My colleague sitting on the adjacent table was looking at me intently, while drinking from a cup.

"Is something wrong, Claudette?" he asked.

"Nothing," I replied.

"You seem to be lost in your thoughts."

I sat down. "Actually, there's this student of mine who ... who ..."

"Who what?"

I've always been good with words, but now I seemed to have lost them. "This student just ... just disturbs me. Yes, that's the word. Disturbing. He's disturbing me."

"Disturbing in what way?" My colleague is a Psychology major so I understood his need for clarification. He put down his cup and gave me his full attention.

"He keeps looking at me in class."

"Everyone looks at the teacher in class. You should be happy because it's a good sign they're listening."

"He looks at me differently. I can tell it's different because I'm not comfortable with it."

"Did you ask him why he's looking at you that way?"

"No. He can always deny it. Then I'll come out as imagining things."

"How about the note? Is that from him? You can ask him about it."

Taking the cue, I arrived at the university early the next day. Walking along the corridors, I felt light and pleasant. Is it the morning breeze scattering fragrance from the Sampaguita patch near the gate? Is it the way the sunlight shines on the glass window producing a kaleidoscope of colors? Is it the smell of newly-cut grass or the sound of cheerful chatter?

As I entered the faculty room, I felt a tug at my belly. I saw a familiar figure standing next to my desk. Tall with broad shoulders. I think his shoulders are too broad for his age, making him appear very manly. He had his back turned and was talking to someone else. I walked slowly, drawing near, hoping not to make any noise as I approached.

I caught his voice asking about my class schedule. "Good morning, I just would like to ask if Ms. De Jesus is coming in today? I think she has a class at eight thirty?"

"Good morning, Mr. Consignado," I greeted softly.

He swung around to face me. Those tawny eyes locking into mine.

"Ms Claudette ... Good morning."

I bid him to pull a chair. As he took his seat, I took out his hand-written note from the folds of my diary.

"There's this note on my desk yesterday ..."

He was listening intently.

"You wrote, 'All I ask is a break.' What exactly do you mean?"

"I was ... I was hoping you'd consider my request to take the exams in the afternoon," he said flatly, seemingly anticipating my refusal.

"You're a varsity player."

"Yes, I'm the team's forward."

I allowed a few minutes of silence before continuing.

"All right. After some thought, I think you can take the exams in the afternoon."

"Thank you. Thank you!" In his exhilaration, he grabbed my hand and gave it a squeeze. His smile was radiant; his eyes like the sun.

After that incident in the faculty room, I never saw Nathan again. He had passed the course and graduated and I was back to my happy (almost!) old self, living alone, spending my lazy afternoons reading books, playing with Jacuzzi, or just listening to dad's favorite tunes.

This time, Spotify was playing a song from a Julia Roberts' movie:

The smile on your face lets me know that you need me
There's a truth in your eyes saying you'll never leave me
A touch of your hand says you'll catch me whenever I fall
You say it best when you say nothing at all.

I was thinking hard about the magic spark which my friends told me to look out for. I chuckled at the thought of Nathan, his tawny eyes giving me the shivers. I brushed the thought aside. I must have mistaken the spark for the beautiful glitter in his eyes. Besides, how could a woman my age end up with a mere boy? I should stop imagining things, I resolved.

A clank coming from the front gate made Jacuzzi scramble to her feet and run barking loudly towards the gate. I got up and caught a glimpse of the mailman walking away from the gate and the mail sticking out of the mailbox, as if waiting to be taken in.

Since the advent of electronic mails, text messaging, online chats, etc. I wondered if people still send actual mails to send their messages across. Unless of course, these mails were bills or printed subscriptions or legal notices that needed to be served. Seeing the mail sticking out of the mailbox, my hopes were high that it wasn't the latter.

I opened the mailbox and retrieved three pieces of mail. First one was from the investment company, probably informing me of a change in their dividend rates or maybe an update on the value of my funds. The second was from a local cable service company, informing of new monthly plans, asking if I would consider an upgrade. The third was a bit of a mystery because it was different from the previous two. It was a yellow-brown envelope with my name written as *Ms Claudette* as the addressee.

As I opened the envelope, I felt a raw sensation at the touch of the handmade paper. Its texture was rough, its edges uneven but its charm lies in its unrefined features.

The envelope contained a card with a simple inscription:

"A break is all I ask. Please meet me tomorrow, 7:00 p.m. at Café Valerie.

It was unsigned. The note kept me awake that night. My eyes were closed waiting for sleep (I go to bed at the same hour every night since I keep a strict schedule) but my mind couldn't stop thinking. I was having mixed feelings. That yellow-brown note brought back bad memories of the foiled blind dates I had. Is this another one of those dates that my friends had arranged? They sure have strange ways of surprising me. But the message also made me think of Nathan. It felt familiar. It didn't sound cold or distant. It seemed to come from someone who knows me. What if it's from him?

The thought was pulling at my pillow the entire night. It was swimming in my coffee mug during breakfast. It was waving at me through the window during my class. And come lunch, it was sitting on top of my ice cream like cherry after lunch. I couldn't quite take my mind off it.

I called to tell my psychologist-friend about the strange note. He was not a bit disturbed but was even surprisingly delighted.

"That's good. The sender is asking for a break. And you yourself need the break."

"I'm not even sure if it's Nathan. It has been two years. What if it's another of those blind dates which I dread? I don't like this. It's disturbing my peace."

"Then you must meet whoever this person is and get your peace back. When you put a face to the unknown, then you stop guessing."

I went to Café Valerie at 6:30 p.m. hoping to catch the anonymous prankster. When I arrived there, a feeling of lightness came over me again. An air of unexplained elation came sweeping over me that I almost tripped over a protruding floor tile.

I looked up hoping no one caught sight of my clumsiness. But I was wrong. Sitting at a table near the window was Nathan, who obviously saw my blunder. An arm was folded over his chest while the other hand was suppressing a smile.

I tried my best to look as commanding as possible. No student of mine could or should make me feel embarrassed. I walked straight up to him.

"So, it's you who sent me the note." I said coldly as I approached. "Is this a joke or something?"

He stood up as I reached the table.

"It's not a joke. I'm so glad you came. Please take a seat."

"Your card was unsigned," I said with a scoff. "It could have been a note from someone dangerous."

"I'm sorry. I'm just not sure if you'll come if you see my name on the note. I know you're busy. I was just taking my chance if you'd be curious enough to know who sent it. Also I'm not sure if you still remember me. It has been so long."

In my mind I wanted to tell him how I often thought of him, the glitter of his tawny eyes was just too charming to forget.

"You're the student who was asking for a break to take the exams in the afternoon because you have basketball practice in the morning. Fiction writing class. Second semester of 1998, if I'm not mistaken."

His expression was red. I could see color rising up to his ears. I could tell he could not believe the sharpness of my memory. I mused, knowing I am and still is in control.

"Still as sharp as I remember," he muttered with a tinge of embarrassment.

I smiled. His words were music to my ears, food for my ego.

"So where have you been since graduation?" I asked squarely.

"I've just finished my master's degree in creative writing."

"That's good," I said. "Where did you study?"

"University of Iowa."

I was amazed, if not envious. I've always wanted to take a short course or attend a writing workshop there. I just couldn't find the time to send an inquiry or write an application. But he worked on something I wanted and was successful in getting it. If someone's keeping score, I think I lost this round. His tawny eyes were still fixed on me.

I've always been good with words but at that moment, "That's good," was all I could mutter.

After a few more updates over coffee (I wouldn't call them coffee dates), I was relieved to know that Nathan was planning to teach. Why not? With the training he got from the Iowa Writers Workshop, he is most qualified. My logical self was telling me he was seeking my help like a sort of mentor. But my psychologist-friend insists it was something else.

"Go back to the yellow-brown handmade paper. The break he's asking for is another chance. It's like saying, 'Hey, I'm here again. And I want to tell you something. Something I've always wanted to tell you in the past, if you just let me.'"

"No, it's not that. Stop it."

"Claudette, you can't deny it. Maybe you should accept that you are defenseless against this great emotion. It's in your eyes. You're beginning to like this guy."

"Stop it. He's just a boy. We'll look bad together. People might even mistake me for his mother. I'm going home." I picked up my bag and walked away.

"Hey!" he called out from the door. "Perhaps it's a lesson on humility. Do you think no one's good enough for you? You can't be in control all the time. And you have to accept that someone has captured a part of you."

On my next meet-up with Nathan, I began to notice how he had indeed grown to be an attractive young man. At 23, he looked stunningly handsome. His tall frame and wide shoulders could make any woman feel secure and protected. His ruffled hair was characteristically rugged, speaking of an untamed nature that refuses the dictates of convention.

"Have you ever done anything so crazy in your life?" he asked me one time. We were walking on the bay walk with the afternoon sun just starting its descent against the purple hued horizon.

"What?" I asked. The wind was blowing hard. I was trying to keep my hair away from my face so I could barely understand his question.

"I said have you done anything that's really crazy? Something you really couldn't imagine yourself doing?"

"Yes," I answered. In my mind I could see myself doing my usual crazy stuff like sleeping late just to finish a really good story or pigging out on spaghetti and lasagna at Piadina's.

"Like what?" he asked.

I looked at him. He had stopped walking and was gingerly looking at me, waiting to hear my answer. I looked down at my sneakers. They were as red as I felt. The tips of my ears were burning.

I looked at him again. This time he was smiling.

"I hate it when you make me feel red in the face." I told him bluntly.

"Do I have that effect on you?" he asked teasingly.

To get back on focus, I opted to answer his question.

"As you were asking about crazy things I did, well, I broke my parents' curfew one time, for which I was grounded. I was so stubborn I ran away and slept in a friend's house for a week."

"For a week?" He repeated the phrase, sounding incredulous.

"Or maybe just a few days, I don't quite remember." I replied.

"That's not so bad," he said.

"How about you?" I asked.

It took him a few moments before he continued. "I fell in love with someone before but everybody's saying I was too young for her. So I tried to love someone my age. And God knows I tried. I made the mistake of getting into one relationship after another only to realize my heart couldn't rest until I knew what had become of her. Imagine all these years, I was still thinking of her. Isn't it foolish?"

"Yes but we all learn from our foolish ways, don't we?"

"What do you think I should do?"

I was not ready to answer his question. My heart was thumping irregularly. I was almost choking at my shortness of breath.

"Perhaps you should see her," I fumbled at the words.

"Do you think I'm old enough for her?"

"Young or old, it doesn't matter. Do you think it matters to her?"

"Does it?"

"What?"

I couldn't remember how our conversation ended. That night was the longest night. I was bewildered. Surprised. Shocked. Stunned. Astonished. I felt as if my world just stopped because a great boulder was getting in the way of its axis.

My life then was simple, living alone in a house with a piano. I loved books and Italian pasta. I did my groceries alone. I liked to listen to love songs. I cried when I remember my mother being killed and I cried even more when I remember my father dying of a broken heart. I had no one else but Jacuzzi to cuddle with. I followed a strict schedule. I had always been in control of my life. But for the first time, I was confused. My schedule was disrupted. Instead of going home after work, I'd stop by Café Valerie to meet this Nathan boy. This boy who had grown to be a man. A man who had shared with me his thoughts and feelings. A man at whose nearness I shuddered for no logical reasons at all. A man who evoked the deepest feelings of elation, bliss, joy, and wonderment. A man whose company I had begun to enjoy. And sometimes I yearn to be with.

It was one o'clock in the morning. My eyes were closed but my mind was still thinking, like shuffling the pages of a book—desperate for answers. Even if my rational mind was against it, I decided to ring my psychologist-friend.

"I'm sorry to disturb you but I need to talk. Nathan was ..."

"Was what? Disturbing you again?" came the croaky voice newly awakened from sleep.

"No he was past that. He was ..."

"Was what?"

"He was confusing me."

"Go to sleep. You've been confused since he came back."

"Please, please don't hang up on me."

"What do you want me to say?" he snapped.

"Tell me what he meant when he said those words."

"I think he likes you. Now go to sleep."

"How about any deeper feelings?"

"You already have the idea in your head. I don't know why you need someone else to say it for your hearing pleasure." He gave a big yawn.

"I need to hear what you think. I'm not thinking straight."

"Women, oh women. Can't live with them, can't live without them. Okay what do you want me to say?"

"Your honest opinion."

"Okay, listen. The next time you meet him, ask him point blank. He always embarrasses you, right? He sets your ears red all the time with those vague statements. Then why not throw in the big question?"

"What's that?"

"ARE YOU TRYING TO TELL ME SOMETHING?"

"I can't say that! He can always deny it. Then I'll come out as imagining things."

"Well, are you imagining things?"

"No. I'm inferring everything from him, from his actions."

"Then get him to clarify your inferences."

"But sometimes he doesn't even say anything."

"So how do you know about these things?"

"I don't know. He has a way of speaking without words. You'll see it in his eyes, his actions, his touch, his ways. He has a way of making me feel he cares about me."

"So what do you intend to do?"

"Ask him perhaps?"

"That's what I've been telling you."

"Okay. Okay. I think I'll do that if I find the courage. Thanks. You can go back to sleep. Thanks really. You're an angel."

The next time I met Nathan, we agreed to meet at the bay walk for an afternoon stroll. With the sun creating beautiful colors in the sky, and the wind blowing not as hard, I think it was the perfect moment to ask him.

I intended to ask him point blank what his intentions were as my psychologist-friend had recommended. But I froze when he reached for my hand and held it. It came so spontaneously for him yet felt so awkward for me that I stopped walking. He looked at me, still not letting go of my hand.

"You're holding my hand," I said, stating the obvious.

"Yes," he replied.

We resumed our walk. I was silent. The feel of his soft fingers, his steady palm against mine was electrifying. There was warmth forming between our hands clasped together. A few minutes more, I stopped again.

"Is there something wrong?" he asked.

"You've been holding my hand ..."

"You don't want me to hold you?" he asked. "Or you don't want people to see me holding you?"

"Nathan," I began, wondering how to address the situation. "I used to be your college professor. You used to be my student. We're what—ten, twelve years apart. We shouldn't be holding each other's hands."

He still wasn't letting go of my hand. Instead, he cupped it with his other hand.

"Do you think I'm too young to hold your hand?" His tawny eyes were locked onto mine.

"No, I think it's me. I'm older. I shouldn't be thinking of myself. I should be thinking of you. I should be protecting you from your emotions and not let you get carried away. It's not proper."

"It is not proper because people will be talking behind our backs? You're afraid of taking the risk, aren't you?" he concluded.

"I don't know." I looked away, thinking of any logical thing to say. Finally I asked, "Tell me, why do you want to hold my hand?"

He smiled, his hand still holding mine. "Remember the woman I told you about. The one I love and the one I thought wasn't for me? You told me to come back for her and I did. Now I don't know how to tell her my true feelings, except that I want only one thing – to hold her hand."

I looked around, wondering if there were any people who could see us. I could not look directly into his eyes, but he was unfazed. "She is very good with words. She writes smoothly like water gliding, washing over me. She is smart, witty, and charming. But she hates risks. Always on the safe side. Always in control. I don't know if I can get the right words to express my feelings for her. She loves music but I can't sing. I can't even play an instrument. So one cloudy afternoon, while walking along the bay walk, I just held her hand, hoping she might feel what's inside me."

Nathan said those words so perfectly I found myself almost in tears. He did not have to prove himself because he had taught me a great lesson on love and how to accept its embrace.

Sometimes we express our feelings through words. Those who are at a loss for words express what they feel through music. But when words and music fail, the heart will find a way to let the other know. Because it has always known right from the very start.

FIREBUGS

Arlo Z. Graves

EMMA WIPES HER EYES on the inside of her shirt as she drives. The twilight sleet on the windshield and the tears turn the winding forest road into a black, twisting snake. A sob squeezes Emma's chest and throat. "Get it together," she orders herself.

But how can she? Thoughts of Owen consume her. What did he see in that other girl?

"What did I do?" Emma whispers. She sniffles and wipes her sleeve through the steam on the windshield.

The terrarium of hissing cockroaches in the passenger seat provides no answer. The drizzly weather has the bugs hiding out in their mossy den. Emma hopes the weather in River Bend won't be too chilly for them.

Owen. Did their three years together mean nothing? Should Emma forgive him?

Should Emma give him a second chance?

No time to dwell on that now. She'll be in River Bend soon. The winter quarter at Redwood University starts in just a few weeks. Transferring to Redwood and moving to Aunt Edith's had been Emma's dream since she graduated high school. Now, without Owen, even the drive feels like a burden.

Emma hears a small hiss from the passenger seat and sets a hand on the glass terrarium. The seat belt holds it in place. Emma takes a shaking breath. "It's okay, we'll be there soon ... Aunty Edith has a heater for you ..."

What can Emma do to win Owen back? His absence yawns like a crater inside her. They had so many plans ...

The deserted, snaking Waterfall Highway veers in a hairpin. Emma brakes. The back end of the Camry fishtails.

"Oh!" Emma pushes the break, but the car keeps sliding, sliding. "Oh shi—!"

•   •   •

Rasping. Harsh, wheezing breaths. Emma can hear herself breathing. Colors flash against her eyelids, reds, blues, the light stabs her brain.

A voice speaks to Emma, earnest and concerned. "We're here with you, you're going to be okay. What's your name, hon?"

Emma squints her eyes open. A face swims into focus, leaning into the window of the Camry. Blue and red flashes over the kind, worried face. "What's your name, hon?"

"Emma ..." croaks Emma. Who is this? What happened?

"Emma, you've been in an accident but you're going to be okay. The ambulance will be here any minute now. Everything's going to be okay."

Ambulance? Emma closes her eyes. What does that word mean? The inside of her head buzzes like bees.

"I've never been ... in a car accident ... never been in a car accident before ..." slurs Emma.

"Well, there's a first time for everything, hon. You're a lucky ducky, just skimmed a tree and bounced off!"

Emma's teeth chatter. Sirens wail in the distance.

"There they are!" says the kind voice. "Emma? We're going to get you out of there now."

Next Emma knows, she lies on her back, staring up into a black forest. Strobing red and blue paints the night. She blinks and finds herself inside a tight, bright space. Voices chatter all around her.

A big figure sits beside Emma. Big, broad, yellow brown and reflective in places. Emma can make no sense of it. The kind face smiles down at her, strawberry blond hair hanging loose and sweaty. A strong hand holds hers.

"You're going to be okay, Emma. Everything's okay now."

Emma believes her. A mask presses over her mouth and nose and the world fades out.

•   •   •

"Emma? Oh, good god. Emma ..."

Emma's eyes squint open at the familiar drawl of Aunt Edith.

Edith stoops over the bed and clasps Emma's hand. She curls her lanky frame onto the side of the bed. "I should have gotten you myself. When I saw the storm coming in ... you're not used to wet country roads ..."

"What happened?" whispers Emma.

"You slid off the road. It's just a concussion, they tell me. Thank god. Oh, thank heaven ..."

Emma looks down at the tubes taped to her arm. Where did the girl go? There had been a girl, right? She must have been ... one of the people who goes to accidents. Emma can't recall the word.

Closing her eyes, tears leak down Emma's cheeks.

"Oh Emma." Edith kisses Emma's hand. "Everything's okay. We'll be able to go home soon. It's all okay."

It's not okay. That much Emma knows at least. Owen's gone. Her life's in smoldering ruins. Three days ago, she had the whole world before her. Today, Emma isn't sure she'll ever be okay again.

•   •   •

Emma lies in bed, eyes half closed and unfocused. It's been two days since she spent the night in the hospital. Her skull still feels too heavy for her neck to hold up and like foam fills the inside. She finds herself dozing off and startling awake.

The only good thing about a head injury is she doesn't have the mental bandwidth to dwell on Owen, the cheating jerk.

She rolls to face the wall, long dark brown hair twisting around her neck. Out the window of her little room in Edith's cabin, a morbid grey sleet dims the forest. It weeps down the window glass.

"Emma, you have visitors." Edith's voice calls from the bottom of the stairs.

Owen? Emma pushes herself up, heart in her throat. Did he come to see her after the accident? She holds on tight to the banisher to wobble downstairs and to the door where Edith waits, hair in a bandana, smile incandescent.

A pair of large, brawny people about Emma's age wait on the porch, a man with a chiseled nose and shoulders as wide as the door frame and a woman nearly as broad with thighs that could crush skulls. They both wear blue shirts with the River Bend Volunteer Firefighter logo on the chest. Neither visitor is Owen.

Emma's heart squeezes and sinks.

The young woman grins. Strawberry blonde hair frames her rounded cheeks. She holds a large glass terrarium in her arms. Her lip gloss sparkles.

"Emma Bridge?" asks the large girl. She has a low, lovely drawl.

"You can come in, you know," quips Edith. She turns to Emma. "They're the Klash twins. They do tree work for me from time to time. I'll make a pot of coffee."

The big Klash siblings kick off their Docs and make their way inside. The girl turns sideways to fit the terrarium through the door.

"Emma … we had to get a new enclosure for your little guys. Yours got cracked. And I hope you only had three … because three's what we found …"

"They hiss!" states the boy, shrugging out of his coat. His arms are bigger than Emma's leg.

The Klash girl looks down into the cage. "The internet said to feed them veggies and dog kibble. I hope that was okay."

"Okay?" Emma blinks. Her mouth cracks open. "You what? You saved my cockroaches?"

"They ... they're pets, right?" The girl holds the cage tighter. "You're not going to feed them to anything ... right?"

"No, of course not. I've had them for years! My old ladies ..."

"Okay good." The girl sets the cage down on the coffee table and offers her hand to Emma. "Camilla. Just Cam. I hope you don't mind us checking in. As you heard, we know Edith."

"They're at the university too!" calls Edith from the kitchen.

Cam's big, calloused hand gives Emma's a definitive shake.

"I graduated, actually," states the boy. He offers his hand once Cam lets go. "Noah."

"Emma ... obviously." She follows the hand up his arm to his startling amber eyes. "How ... how did you get my hissers?"

"They're River Bend volunteer firefighters," Edith carries mugs of coffee into the living room.

Emma's eyes track to Cam. The large young woman kneels beside the cockroach enclosure, talking softly to it. She was the person who held Emma's hand that night.

Edith guides Emma into a cushioned chair and places a steaming mug in her hands. Emma looks into the creamy coffee, mind fuzzing up again.

Edith talks with the Klash siblings, light conversation and laughing. Emma catches Cam glancing her way.

"You look tired, hon," says Cam. She stands. "We should let you rest. Concussions are no joke. Even little ones. Thank you for the coffee, Edith." She steps to the door.

Noah stands as well. He turns a heart-melting smile on Emma. "We're going kayaking in the reservoir next week. If you're up for it, you should come."

"Oh. Okay ..." stammers Emma.

Edith gives the twins a few moments after the door closes before rounding on Emma and propping her fists on her hips. "Honor student. Volunteer first responder. Bug savior. Single." She folds her arms, voice as dry as Death Valley. "I'm not trying to set you up, but come on Em. Come on. Owen wouldn't even go hiking with you."

Owen. Emma sets her coffee aside and lies down on the couch. In the new glass enclosure, one of her elder roaches ventures from the hide. Her antenna wave.

Edith gathers the used mugs. "I know you were high school sweethearts or whatever, and it's hard to see it now, but you're so much better off without him."

•　　•　　•

"Can I give Cam Klash your number, so I don't have to play secretary?" Edith calls up the stairs.

Emma sits on the edge of her bed. Her largest hissing cockroach, Betty, crawls over her palm. "Sure."

Emma watches Betty's segmented body march up her forearm, antenna inspecting the path. Owen hated bugs, especially roaches. He'd once threatened to step on Betty if Emma had her out while he was over. *He didn't mean it,* Emma assures herself.

Emma's phone chimes. She swipes the screen to see a new text message.

> Hi Emma! This is Camilla from last week. Firefighter and bugsitter extraordinaire! We're going kayaking tomorrow.
> If you're feeling up to it, we'd love for you to join us!

Emma remembers Noah's shoulders, nearly as wide as the doorframe. Maybe Edith had a point. Besides, Emma hadn't left the house since the hospital. She types a reply.

> I'd love to!
> Great! 11am tomorrow, I'll pick you up. Dress warm!

Emma opens Instagram and searches out Camilla Klash. The grinning young woman appears in her volunteer firefighter uniform, strawberry blonde hair curling out from under her helmet. It wasn't just the head injury, Cam is big. She's probably six two and built like a bulldozer.

A smile threatens Emma's frown. *She could pick me up with one arm.*

No shit, she did *pick you up,* she reminds herself.

Emma skims through Cam's photos before opening Owen's profile. Ice twists in her stomach. She scrolls and scrolls but can't find a single picture of them together. Not the trip to San Diego, not graduation, not Christmas. He's deleted their entire relationship.

With shaking hands, Emma opens a text message to him. What will she tell him? What can she say to make him reconsider? The phone dings. It's Cam again.

What flavor of muffin do you like? Blueberry, orange, lemon poppyseed, cinnamon?

•   •   •

"You didn't specify, so I got one of each flavor." Cam grins on the porch. She holds a pink bakery box from the local shop.

The River Bend signature drizzle still smudges the forest, but Cam beams like the sun.

"The buggies okay?" she asks. She opens the box and presses it closer to Emma.

Emma can't help it, the orange muffin sets her mouth watering. Plucking it from the box, she sinks her teeth in. "Oh heck. Oh, damn that's good ..."

"Yeah, they're the best," agrees Cam.

"Oh, yeah. The hissers are great. I still can't believe you and Noah saved them like that. People usually think they're gross."

"Unusual maybe," admits Cam. She motions for Emma to follow her out to a pickup truck. "I take it, bugs are your thing?"

"Okay, I know it's weird but yeah. I'll be studying entomology at Redwood."

"That's not weird, it's cool!" Cam hops in the driver's seat and pops the passenger door for Emma. The cab smells like pine. "Do you have an idea how you might, you know, use your studies? Adjust the heater however you like, hon."

"Scientific illustration maybe. But I'd really love to illustrate children's books." Emma buckles her seatbelt. She hadn't said her goals out loud to anyone besides the guidance counselor. It makes her feel transparent.

"Bonus points for children's books about bugs?" prompts Cam. She puts the truck in gear and pulls out of the drive.

"Well yeah, absolutely. I'd like to show kids how important bugs are. I've loved bugs since I rescued a tarantula in kindergarten." She eats the rest of the muffin. "Damn. The bakery's in town, right?"

"Yep. But if you like that, you'll love lunch. Gran's making us sandwiches to take to the reservoir and Gran's a retired chef."

"No kidding."

"No kidding. You okay if we stop by my place to pick up the care package? Gran wants to say hi. She wants to meet Bug Girl."

Emma blushes.

"In a good way!" cackles Cam. Her bright laugh brings sunlight to the grey morning. "So, Redwood University, bugs, drawing ... what else?"

"Well ..." Emma trails off. "I'll be living with Edith ... I used to come up here during summer break. I used to love hiking and outdoor stuff."

"No time like the present to get back into it!"

Owen lurks at the edge of the conversation. "So, Cam. You grew up here?"

"Yep!"

Emma tosses out questions to keep the bubbly Cam talking. The truck winds down the mountain. Aunt Edith owns a little parcel way up between the state park and a logging property at the top of Waterfall Highway. It takes about ten minutes of driving before they see other houses.

Cam pulls into the drive of one of those first rural homes. "This is us! Come on in." Cam leaves the muffins on the seat for the next leg of the trip. She opens the door of the large, two story home. The Christmas tree still crowds one corner of the living room. A pile of grocery bags blocks the hall into the kitchen.

Cam inhales, expression snapping from giggly to horrified. "Gran! Grandma! You didn't drive to town ...!"

"You weren't going to have any lettuce for those sandwiches if I didn't!" calls a voice from the kitchen.

"Oh my god oh my god ... she doesn't have a license ..." whisper screams Cam, grasping Emma by the arm. Louder, she chides: "Gran! You should have waited! I could have driven you!"

A fierce old woman with wild curls shuffles out of the kitchen with a knife. "And then you'd be late! Noah already took off like a bat out of hell. Oh hello! You must be the bug girl!"

Emma can't help it, she smiles. "That's me."

"Gran, you can hardly see, what if you hit someone? Wrapped the car around a tree?" Cam huffs, distressed.

Gran pats Cam's big arm. "Then you'd be there to save me, dear. Pays to have so many first responders in the family." She tosses Emma a gratuitous wink. "Give me just a moment, your lunch is almost ready."

•　　　•　　　•

"I still can't believe her. Driving. Driving!" Cam pulls the pickup into a lot. Below, the reservoir makes a silver mirror of the sky. Emma holds the cold pack of sandwiches and muffins on her lap. Tendrils of fog roll over the dark, glassy water.

Cam grabs another muffin before hopping out, so Emma does likewise.

Noah mills around beside a second pickup truck, two kayaks already unloaded, life vests on top. "Hi Emma!" he waves.

Emma looks him over, from big, generous smile to casually tight jeans. She tucks her chin. "Hey."

A group of three college age men wave from the boat launch. "Ready?" asks Noah.

Cam grins. "You bet!"

Noah lifts the front of the single seat kayak. "Hey, the guys and I are going to head up the creek a little. Water's a bit choppy. You ladies okay with the two-seater?" He slides his eyes between Cam and Emma.

Emma's heart feels just a tad heavier. He doesn't want to sit with her. *Dude, you just met!* She reminds herself.

"Could you give me a hand, hon?" asks Cam.

Emma grabs the back of the kayak and they carry it to the water. Cam helps her in and gives her a quick lesson on how to paddle. Cam sits behind Emma, and Emma can feel her body heat through her sweater.

The kayak slides into the water. Emma holds her breath, letting the moment envelope her as Cam guides them into a dark and narrow ravine. Thick ferns lean over the water.

Emma's breath floats on the air. "This is like a movie set."

"Isn't it pretty?" whispers Cam. "I like to come out here and think. People can't get to you out here. No one's telling you stuff, no one's making you feel bad about anything.

Emma looks over her shoulder. It's hard to imagine anyone making Cam feel bad or why.

They paddle around in companionable quiet until Noah and his rowdy friends join in.

"Hey, are you the bug girl?" calls a tan fellow.

Emma squeezes the paddle in her fists, bracing for teasing.

"I used to have giant millipedes!" he hollers, bouncing off Noah's kayak.

"Oh ..." says Emma.

Cam snickers. "Yeah, you're not the only bug buddy around these parts."

Emma takes a breath. "I guess I'm just ... used to Owen making a whole thing out of it. He hates bugs."

"Owen?" asks Cam. She paddles them out into the lake toward another, wider ravine.

"My boyfriend. Well, ex ... I think."

"You think?"

"He well. He cheated on me but I'm not sure if it was serious."

"Oh hon. It doesn't matter if it was serious. He obviously didn't take *you* seriously. Screw him."

Emma stiffens.

Cam tosses her hair. "There's a whole bug club at school. You're going to fit right in. You're better off without him. Get baked, Owen."

Emma pokes her paddle into the water. Would Owen have gone kayaking with her? Would they have had fun out here? She knows the answer.

"He didn't get into Redwood anyway," mumbles Emma.

"See? A good omen," replies Cam.

From time to time, Noah paddles over to join them. He flicks water at Cam and she nearly drowns him.

"Get Emma wet and I'll roll you under!" threatens Cam.

Emma watches Noah's big arms move his little boat through the water like he was made for it. He grins at her but slides out of easy conversation distance.

Cam leans over her shoulder. "I'm starting to feel lunch o'clock, how about you, Emma?"

Emma glances at her watch. It's been three hours!

"Lunch o'clock sounds amazing."

They make for shore and Cam helps Emma out and onto the dock.

"If you could tie the boat off, I'll go get the sandwiches," offers Cam.

Emma leans over to tie the rope to a metal thing on the dock she assumes serves this purpose. Her elbow sends one of the paddles splashing into the water.

"Ah heck." Emma reaches for it. And slips.

Water crashes over her head. She inhales and chokes. Panic claws through Emma as her heavy clothes and clunky boots weigh her down.

A pair of strong hands grab her jacket, heaving her from the water. Snagging the back of her pants, Cam rolls Emma the rest of the way onto the dock. Emma sputters and coughs, startled and shaking.

Cam guides Emma's useless limbs out of her sodden jacket. Emma feels like a puppet. Emma's fingers turn white with cold and likely surprise.

Cam wrings out Emma's sopping wet hair and wraps her in her own wool-lined jacket. It smells like wet sheep.

Big, strong arms hold Emma. Cam is warm, so warm and steady and safe. Emma stops shivering.

Cam rubs her back. "I've got a blanket in the truck. Jeez, you've gotta stop getting yourself into trouble, girl."

Emma giggles. Her teeth clack together. "But you'll be there to save me, Cam."

"Well ..." begins Cam. She huffs and looks away from Emma. "Well ... we should probably get you home, huh? It's awfully cold to be soaked out here."

•　　　•　　　•

"Hey ... I don't want to be weird but let's be friends, okay?" Cam hovers on Aunt Edith's porch. For someone over six feet tall, she still manages to look small and bashful.

Emma's teeth chatter as she grins. "We're already friends, silly. You purchased my loyalty in muffins."

"And sandwiches, don't forget the sandwiches." Cam presses two wrapped sandwiches into Emma's arms. "Gran's snacks are amazing. Now, go get warm before you catch a chill."

Emma smiles, a real, warm smile that lingers on her face all the way upstairs and into the shower.

It's only then she realizes her phone was in her pocket when she fell in the water. It's dead as a rock.

•   •   •

No phone means no Owen. Sure, Emma could email him or reach out over social media, but the phone feels like permission, in a way. After a couple of days, she finds she isn't reaching for her pocket every half hour to see if he's reconsidered.

And then, just like that, her first quarter at Redwood University starts. Emma had ordered all of the necessary books weeks ago and toured the campus several times with Edith, so the adjustment comes easily. It's made more so by similar schedules with Camilla Klash. Three days out of the week, Cam picks Emma up to carpool to class, smile radiant every time she sees her.

"How is it Noah graduated already? Aren't you twins?" asks Emma one morning. She sips the coffee Gran made for them.

Cam keeps her attention on the road. "I needed a few remedial classes to get into Fire Science and Ecology. I'm caught up now. Should only have a year or so to go."

Emma thinks nothing of it. Their mornings together are the best part of her day. Cam also gets Emma back into hiking. She knows the secret local trails, lookouts, and even caves. She takes great care to guide Emma to the most unusual bugs.

Cam and Emma planned a hike one Tuesday afternoon. Without a phone to check in, Emma walks down Waterfall Highway all the way to Cam's house. A quick knock on the door has Gran pulling Emma inside and plying her with cookies.

"Cam's upstairs in her room dear. She won't mind if you join her."

Emma knocks anyway.

"One sec," replies Cam. She opens the door and Emma does a double take at the tired shadows beneath her bright brown eyes.

"Sorry Em, I thought I'd be done by now." Cam holds the door open. John Deere memorabilia, a Wolverine action figure, and Lincoln Logs make Emma chuckle. The chuckle peters out when she can feel Cam's tension. A book lies open on the bed.

"Octavia Butler?" asks Emma.

Cam sinks onto the edge of the bed. "Unfortunately."

Emma lifts the book. "Unfortunately!"

Cam lifts and drops a shoulder. "I'm supposed to have five questions ready for Friday about it. I'm supposed to be on page 200 or something. Lit class."

Emma saves the page on her finger and flips through. "I still don't see the problem ..."

Cam takes a deep breath and hisses air through her teeth. Her eyes stay fixed on the ceiling. "I can't read very well. I'm not stupid! I just ... Gran used to read to me but since the cataract surgery the light makes it difficult and this is my last required lit class ... I couldn't find the audiobook ..."

The bubbly, beefy persona cracks as Cam's eyes turn red from tears.

Emma drops her pack by the door. She flops onto the bed. "I'll read to you."

"No that's ... you must think I'm so stupid ..."

Emma scowls. "How dare you think so little of Bug Girl? Okay, let's see where you are ... Cool cool, you just started. This book's great, by the way ..." She begins to read.

Thoughts of hikes fade away as Emma reads. It takes Cam a while to relax, but she finally lies down on the bed beside Emma, hair flared out around her head, eyes drifting closed as Emma reads. Emma invites herself under the quilt and moves closer for warmth. It feels good to be close to someone. It feels good to do something useful.

"I like when you do the voices," mutters Cam when Emma finishes. It's dark out now, clouds blocking the sliver moon.

Emma's eyes drift to a CalFire poster on the wall. "How did you decided you wanted to be a firefighter?"

Cam rolls to face Emma. "I want to help people. A lot of folks have helped me along the way and ... I want to make sure I pay that back however I can. Pay it forward. You know?"

Emma doesn't particularly know, so she stays quiet.

"Why bugs?" prompts Cam.

"Because the world doesn't work without them and yet we hate them. If we don't think they're beautiful, we think they're scary or gross. I'd like to change that, even for just one person."

"That's helping too, hon."

Emma snorts. "Not like *you*."

"We all face different fires, hon. Not all of them burn."

Emma finds a sticky note and closes the book on it. "I should probably get home."

Cam raises her eyes to Emma's. "You're welcome to stay. If you want. We have extra toothbrushes and stuff. Gran's probably already made dinner. You're welcome here, Emma." She grins. "We like bug girls here."

•   •   •

Cozy winter days blend into reading sessions and study time, hiking in wool sweaters and hot cocoa in the pickup truck. And then it is spring. Suddenly the mountain mornings bloom bright, the first budding wildflowers and Redwood University plasters the halls with advertising for its Spring Formal, a sort of grown-up prom.

Emma wonders if any of the firefighter posse plans to attend. No word yet, she'll ask Cam tonight. She heads to her car for break. The little Camry's paint got torn up, but he's holding together all the same.

Opening one of Gran's sandwiches, Emma wonders if Noah might ask her to the dance. They've hung out a few times together in the group. He seems sweet, considerate, someone Emma should be more enthusiastic about. Right?

•   •   •

"We're planning to go as a group! Fire themed." Cam bounces

as she opens her phone to show Emma the red dress she picked out. "I got it from the thrift shop. Shh."

"Should I match or ...?"

"You could, or you could do you," suggests Cam. She looks Emma over from head to toe. She leans closer. "You should do you."

•   •   •

The afternoon before the dance, Emma assembles her look. She chose a dark grey gown from a Halloween party, practical boots, and a simple updo. A silver charm around her neck depicts an orb weaver spider, and her dangling earrings are iridescent beetle shells. If that's not her, she's not sure what is. She doesn't worry if Noah will find them gross or not, she already knows better.

As she drives herself to campus, Emma's mind wanders. She likes Noah, he's handsome for sure, but she has no clear goal for the night. Will they dance together? Will they kiss?

Is that something she wants?

Cam's bright brown eyes and ever-ready smile flicker through Emma's mind. What would Cam think?

I'll see how it goes, Emma tells herself. *It's okay to let things happen ...*

After three years tethered to Owen, she feels rather free.

•   •   •

"Your earrings are *gorgeous,*" gushes Cam. Their group, dressed in outrageous reds, oranges, and yellows, waits outside the venue hall. Music thumps inside.

"Thanks! You too," replies Emma. She takes in Cam's crimson dress, her lush, strawberry hair, her wide shoulders and muscular arms. "The dress I mean. Wow."

"Again, thrift shop," winks Cam.

Noah chats with his friends a few people over. He wears a deep red suit and burnt orange shirt. When he senses Emma staring, he turns on his shiniest grin.

Emma grins back but stays beside Cam. She's warm and smells of mint.

The venue gets the job done. It's a fundraising event for some campus club, not exactly a gala, but there's a nice selection of snacks, drinks, and treats.

The volunteer firefighters pile into the photobooth for a goofy snapshot.

"Emma, get over here!" calls Cam.

"I'm not ..."

"Bug girl!" the others cheer.

Shaking her head, Emma crouches down in front of the group. Cam wraps her arms around her middle from behind. Emma signs. She should have brought a warmer shrug. Cam's body heat feels so welcome in the brisk hall.

Emma stays with the group for the first hour before breaking off to chat with a girl in her intro to entomology class. When the girl excuses herself to hang with her volleyball friends, Emma makes her way to the cookie buffet. Noah's back faces her from the drink table. His wide back and orange shirt makes a striking statement piece.

"Hey," Noah greets her, grin immaculate.

Emma closes the distance between them with a step. "Hey back."

A ballad begins to play, something slow and longing.

"Uh-oh." Noah tosses back the rest of his Sprite and offers Emma his hand. "Don't want to be caught on the sidelines ..."

Emma takes the hand and lets him lead her onto the floor. His big hand rests on her back. She looks up into his brown eyes.

"How's River Bend treating you?" asks Noah, just loud enough for Emma to hear. The hand on her back pulls her closer.

"Good," replies Emma. "Well. I like it. It's nice."

He cocks his head. "Just nice?"

"I mean, there are some special highlights."

Noah doesn't reply. They slow dance, close but not too close.

Get closer, Emma goads herself. *Now's as good a chance as any girl ...*

Noah's big, strong frame guides her through the sway of the dance. Emma's heart throbs in her throat but her eyes drift to the side. Cam hovers at the drink station, crimson dress shaped to her curves like cling-wrap. Warmth spreads through Emma, a deep, sweet warmth that reaches the tips of her fingers.

Cam turns, her hair sweeps back over one broad shoulder. Her eyes shine as they lock with Emma's.

Oh.

Oh no.

The song ends. Emma wobbles back from Noah and she hooks a thumb over her shoulder. "Bathroom," she stutters. As soon as she reaches the hall, she runs to her car, lurches out of the lot, and speeds for home.

•   •   •

The sound of Emma's breath rasps in her ears as she drives. *Oh my god. Oh my god ...*

She makes it all the way to Waterfall Highway before it clicks in her head that she left without telling anyone. *You're being an idiot. You need to go back ...*

Pulling into a turnout, she turns around on the dark, deserted road. As the Camry picks up speed, she catches a flicker of light. Headlights swerve around a corner, a dark car fishtails.

Emma pulls over and throws on her hazard lights. In the rearview mirror, she can see the taillights of the other car sitting perpendicular in the road. It is a familiar car.

Emma hops out and her throat tightens. She indeed knows that car.

"Gran?" calls Emma. "Mrs. Klash, are you okay?"

"Oh Emma, is that you?" Gran squints out the window at her. Her voice trembles. "I didn't think my eyes were so bad. The headlights nearly blinded me ..."

"Gran ... you're not supposed to be driving." Emma takes a knee at the window. The car seems alright, it didn't hit anything, thank goodness. "Scoot over, I'll take you home."

Gran gets out and moves to the passenger seat. "Aren't you kids supposed to be at the shindig? You didn't leave with Camilla?"

Emma's face burns. "I ... I'll call her as soon as we get you home. I just ... the dance was a lot."

Emma stays silent for the rest of the drive, pulling the car safely into the Klash residence. She sits for a moment with her hands on the wheel. What if she hadn't run off? Would Gran have made it home? *The important thing is, she is home,* Emma reminds herself. She helps Gran inside.

"I still can't believe my vision's that bad ... this could have been bad if you weren't there."

"It's okay, everything's okay now." Emma holds onto the keys just in case. She'll give them to Cam. "Hey, Gran? Do you think I could use your phone for the walk back to my car?"

Gran passes it over. "Of course, dear. What a night."

Emma hugs herself as she walks down the shoulder of Waterfall Highway. A cold fog settles in around her, grey as her dress. She unlocks Gran's phone and dials Cam. *What are you going to say?*

Cam picks up on the second ring. "Gran?"

"Cam?" says Emma when she picks up. "It's Emma ... Cam I ... Cam. Can you meet me out on Waterfall Highway?"

"Is Gran?"

"Grans fine. She was out driving and ... well, she's home safe now."

"God. I'll be there as soon as I can," replies Cam. She hangs up.

Emma keeps hugging herself. Her heart pounds in her ears and her stomach clenches. *What are you going to say?*

A thrill shoots up Emma's spine each time headlights flash in the distance—part fear, part something else. Then the familiar pickup truck pulls over.

Cam turns on her hazard lights and leaps out. "Emma! I saw your car, what in the world ...?"

Emma stutters through an explanation, about nearly hitting Gran on the road.

"Oh my god, oh my god ... she can't be out like that ... you might have saved her, Em ..." Cam paces. Then she stops and turns to Emma. She leans against her truck. "Em ... why'd you leave? Are you okay?"

Emma can't get enough air into her lungs. "I was dancing with Noah and ... I guess I panicked."

"That bad, huh?" quips Cam. She grins, but it doesn't reach her eyes.

"No I ... I ..." *What are you going to say?* "I think I was dancing with the wrong person." She lifts her eyes to Cam's. Her face burns. "Maybe the wrong twin ..."

Cam's confused expression softens. Her lips part on the beginning of a sentence, but all she says is: "Oh."

"I ... I'm sorry ..." Emma looks at the ground. "I'm sorry."

"Oh." Says Cam. She scuffs her shoe in the gravel. "I'm not. I'm nuts about you."

That warm, sweet thrill rises through Emma again. Her breath becomes a scared little giggle. "You are?"

"Come here." Cam pulls the shivering Emma into her big, warm arms. The tension melts from Emma, a sigh leaves her. She allows herself to melt into the hug, to wrap her arms around Cam's tough, strong body. Strawberry blonde hair tickles her face.

Cam leans back enough to cup Emma's chin in her calloused hand. "If you think you've got the right twin now, may I kiss you, bug girl?"

Emma inhales. "I've never kissed a girl before," she says.

Cam smiles. Her brown eyes shimmer in the foggy dark. "There's a first time for everything."

MY WAY BACK TO YOU

Denise Lee

A SOFT AND INVITING SMELL wafted through the open window on the porch. Through the slight opening in the window, the sound of laughter added to the warmth. Joshua stood outside of this house. He stood there, staring at the closed door. In his hands, he held a bouquet and a small weightless box rested in his pocket.

With a sigh, Joshua thought to himself that maybe he should finish what he came here to do. He came here to apologize to his girlfriend, Penelope. This was the make-up after the break-up. They had a slight argument about Joshua's career. Well, it started as a slight argument that blew up into them breaking up which was neither's intentions when they began. Penelope's concern started with Joshua leaving her every few weeks because he had to fly out with his team. As a hockey player, Joshua was always traveling with the team to away games and, as a crucial player on the team, he needed to be there. A good portion of his games were in different cities, states, and sometimes Canada. Unfortunately, Penelope had a fear of airplanes, so she often wasn't with him on these trips. Their time together would always be short because of this, and Penelope would always tell him how much she missed being around him.

But this wasn't the end of Penelope's concerns about Joshua; much to his chagrin. She also disliked his style of play. Joshua is a physical player in the sport of hockey. He liked to cause fights and be the instigator. Joshua is often the first to land a hit on his opponents and he's always eager to grind for possession for his team. As one of the top players on the team, he felt the responsibility to play this role for his team. So Joshua tried to dispel this. He explained that he'd played this way since he was a kid, so changing to another style of play proved too difficult for him as he had tried before he met Penelope. Penelope had her own counter to that; Joshua always had a fresh injury that he would hide from her. Penelope often warned him that these injuries would pile up on him and he might regret always putting himself on the line. Joshua remembers scoffing at that, saying he can handle that as he always did before he met her. But instead of stopping there, Penelope responded by saying that she couldn't handle that and he should consider her at least sometimes when he plays.

This irritated Joshua. Getting into the physical side of play shows heart, it shows commitment and passion for the sport and the team. Joshua is the player on the team known for his strength and grit. It helped him get drafted to become one of the star players in the league. It was a sense of pride for Joshua. This accusation from his girlfriend, of all people, offended him. Penelope just didn't understand that, so he told her that maybe they shouldn't be together if she couldn't take that. He figured that would've expressed how much he didn't like that suggestion. Offended that he would even suggest breaking up, Penelope agreed. Maybe they shouldn't date; it would save her some heartbreak at least.

Joshua remembers seeing her walk away from him after that. The hurt that lashed across her face. Her tears welling up in her eyes before she turned away; the force of her turn whipping her hair back behind her. And her angry footsteps, so quick and heavy. The feeling of seeing her walk away sunk sourly in the pit of his stomach. He recalled thinking that he shouldn't have said that and he knew better than to create a divide between them, but he still did. Joshua took their argument farther than it should have gone. He knows that now. However, it took him weeks of feeling and hearing her absence to realize that she only cared.

It started out just missing her voice. Penelope had a voice that was warm, deep, and smooth. She had a raspy quality to her voice that was natural. As a singer, it was noticeable when she sang. Her voice was one of the many things Joshua adored about Penelope. The way it felt as if a blanket warmed by the fireplace draped itself across his sore shoulders after a rough game gave Joshua ease. Next, it was her thoughtfulness. Penelope would always check in with Joshua over the phone after any game. She'd ask about his performance and how'd he'd rate it; as if she didn't watch the game at home or in the stands. Joshua found this to be the cutest quality about her. Last, her presence. He missed having her around. Penelope is a bubbly and sweet person in contrast to his mellow and chill personality. They were a good balance for each other.

Joshua looked down at his hands. His bouquet of yellow daisies glared back at him; just like Penelope would. Her favorite flower. His other hand fidgeted with the velvet box. Joshua's eyes turned to the door in front of him. Penelope's parents lived here. She would visit them every other weekend because she was quite close to them. It was a new tradition of hers, as in her eyes, calling them on the phone just didn't do it. Joshua knew she'd not appreciate him showing up unannounced and bringing their relationship drama to her parents' door, but she was ignoring his attempts at reconciliation. He knew Penelope was ignoring him on purpose but he wanted to talk things out for real this time; no arguing.

Joshua knew Penelope's parents loved him, too. Her mom had his phone number, and they'd talk about Penelope all the time. Her dad is a big hockey fanatic, and he'd talk about hockey with Joshua for hours if Penelope left them alone together. Thankfully, she never did. Joshua had his limits on these discussions and the man couldn't take the hint.

Another sigh escaped Joshua. How long was he going to stand here and contemplate? It was time to put his plan in motion. He wanted to apologize to Penelope. That he should've done better. She is an important person to him and she should feel that from his actions, not feeling left behind because of his hurt pride. Joshua raised his hand to knock on the door.

"Josh, what are you doing here?"

An exasperated voice sounded from his left. Penelope came out from the open garage and onto the walkway leading to the front porch. She stood with her arms folded and her stance guarded. She was not happy to see him. Penelope tapped her foot on the brick tiled walkway as she stared down Joshua; her stare feeling like freshly sharpened needles digging into his thoughts.

Penelope wore a bright yellow sundress patterned with daisies. Her dark hair pinned up high off her neck with a few stray strands blowing in the light breeze. Penelope fixed her round rimmed glasses on her face a couple of times as she waited for Joshua's excuse despite knowing it won't be enough to explain his intrusion on her trip to her parent's house.

Joshua stepped off the porch and walked halfway down the walkway between the flowerbed of daisies in front of the porch and the front lawn until he was in front of Penelope. Not close enough to touch her, though; he kept a respectful distance. Joshua hid his flowers behind his back, even though he was sure she saw them, and opened his mouth to begin his excuse when Penelope abruptly cut him off.

"If you're not sincere, I do not want to hear it, Josh. I mean it."

Hearing her say that, Joshua had to rethink his words. He considered saying something Penelope wanted to hear. However, maybe he should say what's on his mind instead. His shoulders held so much tension; he was sure they rested next to his ears and felt stiff as wood. He ground his teeth together and clenched his jaws in frustration.

"Penny, I came here to talk ... with you."

"Talk? What do we need to talk about? There's nothing to talk about, Josh. We aren't together anymore, therefore, nothing to say, yeah?"

Her words clipped. Penelope's foot tapped. Her eyebrows furrowed together and her lips thinned into a straight line.

This was harder than Joshua'd imagined it was going to be. She was very unhappy with him. A deep sigh escaped Joshua again. He understood that through his reckless words, he'd hurt someone he cared for. It left a mark he needed to work to erase bit by bit. If he could at all.

"On that day months ago, you clarified that what happens to you is none of my business. It will not change, and my concerns are irrelevant, right? Because as a hockey player, you can't control yourself when you play. So, we don't need to be together, like you said."

Penelope's volume raised in pitch as she spoke. And, Joshua remembers, now. He'd said she'd annoyed him with her fretting over his injuries. He remembers seeing the hurt on her face. The disbelief that he would say something like that. Almost a kind of betrayal.

"Yes, that's what I said. But I said it wrong. It felt like you were trying to change me-"

"I never would change anything about you, Joshua!"

Joshua could hear the panic in her voice, and he cringed. This wasn't how he wanted this to go. He shook his head. He needed Penelope to know how he felt.

"I know. Penny ... I'm sorry for not taking your fear seriously and not hearing your worry. I'm sorry for the person I was that day. Not gonna blame you if you never want to deal with me again, but for now, I need you to know I am so sorry."

His face felt wet. It wasn't raining. In fact, the sun was shining high in the sky. Joshua was crying. The sorrow he felt for hurting his girlfriend made him cry. Joshua couldn't remember the last time he cried. He closed his eyes and took a deep breath. Joshua recomposed himself, as he still had something to say.

"I know this isn't where you wanted to have this conversation, but I knew you'd be here. You've been ignoring me for good reasons, but I miss you. I miss everything about you, Penelope. I promise that if you decide to forgive me, I will be more considerate towards you. You leaving me had me realize I need you in my life."

Joshua opened his eyes to find Penelope was the one crying now. Her entire demeanor had changed. She no longer had furrowed eyebrows and her shoulders sagged down as if the weight of his words had brought them there. Her hands covered the bottom half of her face. Penelope had gotten closer, too. Just an arm's length distance away. Joshua could smell her perfume; a mix of berries and with a hint of vanilla. She always smelled like her personality - sweet.

The urge to reach out to her was strong, but he needed to resist it. Joshua's hands flexed at his sides. The flowers he held had dropped at some point. He can't recall. All he knew was it was Penelope who needed to tell him if it was okay for him to touch her.

"All I ask is, don't brush me off like that ever again, Joshua."

"You got it."

Both of their voices were hoarse with emotions.

Penelope falls into Joshua's arms. Her knees buckle as she rests all her weight on him and lays her head on his shoulder. She gives no warning. Almost like she knew he'd never drop her. He holds her tight. So tight his knuckles turn white, almost instantaneous. Penelope returns his squeeze like she'd suffocate if she didn't. Neither of them said anything for what felt like hours, but they knew it was only minutes. Penelope was the first to let go. Joshua groans in protest, earning a soft laugh from Penelope. Now that they've separated, they each gaze at each other. Their eyes taking in the appearance of their significant other whom they haven't seen in months.

Penelope changed her hair color. It was a dark chestnut brown and blended in beautifully with her natural curls. Her glasses, also new, gave her a sophisticated feeling that Joshua couldn't get enough of right now. On her lips was a pretty deep rose color, highlighting her cupid's bow shape.

Joshua's green eyes held a darkness to them that Penelope guessed he pick up in the months without her. He also gained slight stubble facial hair despite not being able to grow facial hair at the beginning of their relationship. She noticed the fresh ink of a possible new tattoo underneath the collar of his shirt.

Following her eyesight, Joshua chuckles softly.

"It's a new one. I got it a couple weeks ago, so it's still healing."

Penelope nodded and turned her attention to the sad and forgotten flowers that lay on the brick walkway. But before Joshua could say anything about them, Penelope swooped down to pick them up. A wide, serene smile spread across her face.

"Daisies for the daisy, huh?"

She teased Joshua in a quiet voice; just loud enough for Joshua to hear without straining. Daisy was a nickname Joshua had given Penelope when they just started dating. He claimed she always looked like one, so he believed it suited her. She begged to differ and gave him several reasons she didn't like that nickname for a month straight after; Joshua learned not to call her that anymore with surprising speed. Although, the name became an inside joke between them. He smiled at her teasing.

"Penelope, we should talk about this ... argument we had more. I feel uneasy about it all."

She lowered her flowers from her nose and stared at Joshua. He was never one to admit his anxieties, so this worried her. She knew they had a lot they needed to discuss.

"Yeah, we should, but first, come inside and say hello. Then we'll talk in private, okay?"

Joshua nodded. He missed her parent's, too. When they broke up, they stopped talking to him too.

"Yeah, I'm glad you've forgiven me, but I have this nagging feeling that we might upset each other again if we don't talk it out."

Penelope frowned at Joshua's words. She didn't doubt their make-up was easy, but hearing Joshua say that they may argue again makes her chest tighten and her breathing quicken. Penelope saved her thoughts for the conversation later and walked herself and Joshua to the door.

She twisted the doorknob and Joshua caught the door halfway to open it fully for Penelope. She smiled back at him.

"Penny, is that you? I've been looking for you! I thought you'd left!"

Penelope's mother, Agnes, gasped when she walked into her living room. Joshua stood next to Penelope, rubbing a hand on the back of his neck, looking very interested in studying the pattern on the floorboards. Penelope smiled, showing her teeth at her mother, gesturing at Joshua as she walked to the kitchen to put the flowers in some water.

The Jackson's house has always been inviting for Joshua. He looked around as he hadn't been around for a while and noticed not much had changed. The living room he stood in flaunted its bright colors and patterns in typical Agnes Jacksons' fashion. She also loved daisies, so there were plenty to see both in pattern and live plant. The walls were now a creamy tan that brought some neutrality to the room, different from the light blue he once knew them.

Joshua noticed that Mr. Jackson wasn't in the room; so he peered down the hallway leading out of the living room only to see the back door of the house, lit from the outside in. Joshua knew the bedrooms were back there, so he figured that's where Mr. Jackson was. Not that he'd prepared himself to see him again.

"Joshua! It's so good to see you again! How've you been?"

Agnes stepped to Joshua with purpose and placed a hand on his arm. She gave it a reassuring squeeze.

"I've been doing okay, Mrs. Jackson. I missed you and Mr. Jackson. Penelope, too."

Joshua glanced at Penelope, and they met eyes. She gazed at him in a way that made his nerves jitter. The intensity of her gaze nestled the hole created in him by her absence. Joshua felt every bit of that warmth and wanted nothing more than to return that feeling to her. He concentrated on that feeling. A smile that only he knew the meaning behind inched its way on her lips.

The sound of someone clearing their throat sliced through the room as Penelope's father, Keith, walked in. He noticed how comfortable everyone was. Keith didn't share the enthusiasm of seeing Joshua. He remembered when Penelope and Joshua broke up. Seeing his daughter distraught as she was, Keith hoped she'd take the distance as a chance to heal herself first. So, with Joshua standing in his living room now, confirmed either that didn't happen or she planned to talk that out with him; if he knew his daughter well enough.

Her father wore such a stern and sour expression. His jaw clenched and his eyebrows dipped low. Penelope spoke to her father earlier that day and confessed to him she wanted to talk things out with Joshua. Maybe they both needed to air their grievances first and reconcile later. Keith worked as a therapist all his life and didn't agree with what Penelope wanted to do, but as it's her life, he'd settled with her making these decisions on her own; a point of contention during Penelope's adolescence. Keith needed to let her figure out her relationships by herself.

Sensing the tension brewing, Agnes steps up to diffuse the situation as best she could.

"Keith, honey, it's Joshua. He wanted to see us; even said he missed us. Isn't that sweet?"

Agnes watched her husband's expression as she walked over to him, linking her arm with his. His face gave away nothing of his feelings as he stared at Joshua.

Joshua, still avoiding eye contact, felt the silent displeasure of Keith's stare without looking. Penelope frowned upon seeing how uncomfortable Joshua was getting. This isn't quite how she saw this going.

She stepped in front of Joshua and reached back behind her to grab his hand. He squeezed her hand and intertwined their fingers; grateful for her protection.

"Dad, I know he messed up. He apologized for it and remember, I wasn't perfect either. I told you I asked some things of him that may be hard to fix right away, so I have to apologize too. We'd agreed to talk later in private, as this is our relationship. I've already told you too much as it is. I know you only want to protect me, but I can handle myself."

Keith watched as his daughter created the firm boundary he knew she needed to make. Half her body shielded Joshua from his stare, even though her stature highlighted her much smaller height. He noticed their hands fused together tight, and it took all the tension away as fast as it came. Keith let go of his apprehension, signaling with a nod to Penelope that she was right.

"I understand, dear. You know your ol' dad still thinks of you as his baby girl. Gonna need to get used to that one day."

He chuckles sheepishly as Agnes, Penelope, and Joshua all collectively sigh in relief. Keith always is fiercely protective of Penelope and she, along with her mother, worked to change that, but some of it still lingers. Perhaps as it always will.

"Joshua, I hope I can trust Penelope's confidence in you again. I would hate to lose my hockey buddy."

Joshua looks up at Keith upon hearing this. Keith gives a small smile, and Joshua exhales again.

"I ... would hate that too, Mr. Jackson."

Joshua, feeling better, returns the smile. To him, it felt like going back home. Somewhere he knew even when he screws up, he can return to. A warm and fuzzy sensation settles in Joshua's stomach before he sees Penelope pulling him towards the back door and onto the back porch.

"They're too much, right? Mom tried not to be too nosy, but Dad asked so many questions! I can't lie to him either, because he'll see right through it. I refused to tell him only we argued, and we broke up."

Penelope rested her arms on the railing, and Joshua took a seat behind her on the cushioned chairs. Silence stretched on for minutes. The afternoon sky transitioned into the evening dusk as the partly cloudy sky changed from bright cerulean to a hazy blue. It was the time of day where the temperature lowers; the breeze flows by, and the fireflies dance out of hiding.

Still, the silence persists. Neither wanted to talk. Both knew they needed to, but the thought of the conversation going south gave them pause. Taking a deep breath, Joshua spoke first.

"Is your fear of heights what's keeping you from flying to games? I can help keep you calm when you fly."

His voice was soft as he mentioned the first concern Penelope ever brought to him. His solution then was to not fly with him; he brushed it off. Her presence at his games lifted his mood, and he played with so much fire. Joshua went into those games, wanting to impress Penelope with his skills, so he lied when he said it didn't matter.

"Yes. I've talked to my dad about my fear and he suggested that the more I do something that scares me, the more I'll realize my fear was of the unknown. He said that maybe it was the journey to flying and not the act itself that scares me. You know, classic anxiety."

"So, he's working you through this in therapy?"

Penelope hummed her answer. Her dad, since his retirement, has been her own personal therapist for a couple of months. "I say all that to say ... let me fly with you to your games this season. I want to go to as many as I can."

Penelope feels Joshua turn her around; his hand gently pulls her backwards off of the railing, forcing her to stand straight. She meets his eyes again today and sees a softness to them, like he's so fond of her. Penelope looks away from Joshua's watchful gaze as she feels the heat rush to her cheeks and her heart beat in her ears.

Joshua can't believe what he just heard. Penelope wants to go to his games with him. The woman who cries at the sight of an airplane is now brave enough to travel the country on one. All for him?

"Penny, are you sure? We can have you at, like, one a month until you adjust or something."

"I'm fine, Josh. I want to be there for you like you've been for me. I mean, you were about to let my dad scold you! You hate for anyone to talk to you as if they were your family. I ... haven't ever seen you do that before."

Joshua laughs at her astonishment. She isn't wrong. As an orphan, Joshua grew up with foster parents constantly wanting to change his straightforward attitude, citing it as problematic. He despised the foster parents who would talk to him as if they were his birth parents. While he knew his birth parents for only a short time in his life, he appreciated his adoptive parents, who'd recognized he didn't need that kind of parent. Joshua wanted parents who just treated him like a child.

"That's because they are family, sweetheart."

Now it was Penelope's turn to be surprised. Did Joshua see her as family, too? This creates a whole new dynamic in their relationship. Did he want her to be a part of his family?

"I've thought better about things, too. I asked one of our assistant coaches about my physical play style and how I could marry the physical side with some self-preservation. I told him about you and how worried you've been over my injuries and he gave me some tips during practice yesterday. When I tried them out, I got a lot of positive reactions from teammates."

Joshua put his hands in his pocket as he rocked back on his heels, a flirty smirk on his face. His left hand fiddled with the once-forgotten box in his pocket. So much went on tonight Joshua had momentarily forgotten about the velvet tiny box holding the necklace he bought for Penelope. He traced his sight along her face, studying her reaction to himself.

Penelope's eyes lit up with excitement. She couldn't believe again that Joshua sought a compromise to her concern and his special talent.

"I can't believe that you would do that! I'd given up, unfortunately. Sorry."

Penelope confessed to Joshua. She knew, after thinking about it for months, she'd asked something of him that is a part of his identity; it made him special. With the hockey season so close, Penelope understood he'd changed in so little time. Joshua shrugged.

"I told you earlier. I'd do anything to keep you happy and in my life. I understand losing you wasn't what I wanted, ever."

"Wasn't it hard to just change something that is so fundamental to you as a person?"

"Yes, but it was needed anyway."

Joshua smirked, seeing the slight confusion on Penelope's face. He pulled his hand out and presented her with the box in the palm of his hand. Penelope gasped.

"Joshua, what's this?"

He opened the box to show her the beautiful sparkling rose gold chain necklace with a daisy pendant. Penelope couldn't explain her feelings, no matter how much she tried. Her heart felt so full, bright, and happy.

"Daisy for the daisy, right? I love you, Penelope."

She reached out, her hand shaking, to grab the necklace. Joshua intercepted her, though. He gestured for her to turn around to put the necklace on. Penelope smiled from ear to ear as she turned back towards Joshua, asking him how the necklace looked on her. He laughed and told her she looked beautiful.

She bounced forward one step into his arms as he wrapped his arms around her. Just loud enough for him to hear, she whispered her love back.